THE RIGHT KIND
OF WRONG

By the Author

Visit us at www.boldstrokesbooks.com

THE RIGHT KIND
OF WRONG

by
PJ Trebelhorn

2017

THE RIGHT KIND OF WRONG

ISBN 13: 978-1-62639-771-2

THIS TRADE PAPERBACK ORIGINAL IS PUBLISHED BY
BOLD STROKES BOOKS, INC.
P.O. BOX 249
VALLEY FALLS, NY 12185

FIRST EDITION: FEBRUARY 2017

CREDITS
EDITOR: CINDY CRESAP
PRODUCTION DESIGN: STACIA SEAMAN
COVER DESIGN BY SHERI (GRAPHICARTIST2020@HOTMAIL.COM)

Acknowledgments

As always, my continued appreciation goes to Len Barot, Sandy Lowe, and Bold Strokes Books for allowing me to be a part of this amazing family. I truly enjoy being a part of it!

Appreciation also goes to Cindy Cresap, editor extraordinaire. Thank you for all you do!

To my sister, Carol, thank you for always pushing me to keep writing. I can't put into words how much you mean to me.

Thank you, Sheri, for another amazing cover!

And thank you to you, the reader, for your encouraging messages on Facebook and for the emails I get from you. Without you, none of us would be doing this!

For Cheryl, always

CHAPTER ONE

Quinn Burke had her elbows on the bar, her eyes scanning the room before her. This wasn't a lesbian bar, but there were certainly plenty of them who frequented the place. Brockport, New York, was more or less a college town. Not on the same scale as an Ohio State or a Michigan, that was for sure. But there were more than enough students, of legal drinking age, of course, to keep the joint hopping through the school year.

"How many times do I have to tell you they're too young for you, Burke?" Taylor Fletcher asked as she took a seat at the bar in front of Quinn. Quinn pushed off the bar and grinned as she set a coaster in front of Taylor and got her usual ginger ale.

"I think you need to tell them, not me," Quinn said with a quick grin and slight lift of her shoulder. "I've never once tried to pick any of them up, and you know it."

"Yes, I do," Taylor said before taking a sip of her soda. "But I also know you do very little to discourage them too."

"Seriously?" Quinn asked, unable to hide her surprise. "Are you telling me if a twenty-two-year-old college senior was coming on to you, you'd cast her aside and walk away?"

"You ask that as though you think it doesn't happen to me."

Quinn studied Taylor for a moment, not sure whether or not she was pulling her leg. Taylor owned the bar Quinn had been working at for the past fifteen or so years. Taylor was forty-two, the same age as Quinn. She wouldn't describe Taylor as drop-dead gorgeous as she'd heard more than one patron describe her. But she was definitely attractive, especially in the way she carried herself. Her hair was so dark it was almost black, and her brown eyes were expressive in a way Quinn had never seen before. Taylor Fletcher turned heads whenever she decided to make an appearance in the bar. From men and women alike.

"Oh, I know it happens," Quinn replied. "I've seen it with my own eyes."

"And have you ever seen me leave with any of them?"

"No," Quinn said with a shake of her head.

"You might do well to show some restraint too." Taylor grinned, her tone teasing but nevertheless a challenge to Quinn's ears. Taylor didn't have a problem with her employees fraternizing with the customers so long as it was done discreetly, and away from the bar.

"You don't think I can say no?" Quinn asked as she staggered backward a couple of steps and put a hand over her heart.

"I know you can't." Taylor laughed and leaned back on her bar stool. "Prove me wrong. Turn down the next woman who comes on to you."

"Fine," Quinn said, while at the same time hoping it wouldn't be the blonde who'd been eyeing her all evening. What Quinn wouldn't do with that body pressed against hers. Her gaze automatically went to the young woman in question, and Quinn swallowed hard. She was heading toward the bar. Quinn shot a look of contempt in Taylor's direction and considered asking for a reprieve, but then decided against it. She could do this.

"Hi," the woman said shyly.

"What can I get for you?" Quinn asked, both hands gripping the edge of the bar more tightly than was necessary.

"Funny you should ask," she said with a quick glance over her shoulder in the direction of her friends. Quinn followed her line of sight and saw the other women nodding and waving at their nervous companion. Quinn almost felt sorry for her. "I was wondering what time you get off."

Holy crap, what a loaded question. Quinn could think of any number of witty and flirty responses to *that* question, but she could feel Taylor's eyes boring into her. She shook her head at the young woman, hoping she didn't look as disappointed as she felt at what she was about to do.

"I'm sorry," she said. "I have plans after work tonight."

"Oh," said the blonde, looking seriously defeated. Quinn's fingers twitched with the desire to touch her. "I'm sorry to have bothered you."

"Wait," Quinn said with a quick glance at Taylor, who was attempting to cover a smile by putting her glass to her lips and pretending to take a drink. "What's your name?"

"Chelsea."

"Maybe next time, all right? And believe me, you weren't bothering me." Quinn smiled as she moved to help another customer. "My name is Quinn, by the way."

"How do you do that?" Taylor asked, pointing in the direction of the group of women when Quinn stood in front of her to get a draft beer.

"Do what?"

"Reject her, yet still make her feel better when she walks away than she did when a night alone with you was a possibility in her mind."

"It's a gift." Quinn laughed as she walked away with the beer she'd just gotten for a customer. After taking the guy's money, she returned to Taylor. "I can teach you if you'd like."

Taylor reached across the bar and backhanded her on the arm. Quinn feigned injury and laughed at Taylor's bemused expression. Quinn turned serious though when she caught sight of Grace Everett walking toward the bar. Grace had been her best friend for the past twenty years, and Quinn knew from experience that Grace was upset about something. It was obvious in the way her forehead creased, and she was walking like she was trying to contain her anger and not quite making it.

Taylor seemed to realize it too, and she quickly vacated the seat before giving Grace a kiss on the cheek and retreating to her office. Quinn set a glass of red wine in front of Grace and leaned forward, trying to catch her eye. Not an easy feat considering Grace was staring at her own lap. Quinn placed a finger under her chin and forced her to look up.

"I thought you had a date with Lauren tonight," Quinn said. "What happened?"

"She had to work," Grace answered as she shrugged off her light jacket and flung it over the back of the empty bar stool next to her. It was mid May, and spring still hadn't made much of an appearance in their part of New York. "An *emergency* surgery."

Quinn nodded, knowing exactly what was going through Grace's mind. One of Grace's old girlfriends had been a surgeon, just like Lauren. The problem was, the ex would use work as an excuse to spend time with other women. Quinn knew without a doubt Grace was letting her mind wander back to that time.

"Honey, I've only met Lauren once, but she doesn't seem to me to be anything like Holly," Quinn said. Quinn didn't like Lauren at all. Truth be told, Quinn hadn't liked any of the women Grace had been involved with, but she'd never admit it to Grace. Every one of them had the potential to take Grace away from her and put a wedge between them. Quinn had seen it happen to other friends, and she'd be stupid not to realize it could happen to them too. Juliet, Quinn's ex, had tried to come between them, but Quinn wouldn't let it happen.

She knew enough not to talk bad about the woman her best friend was dating though, because that could cause all kinds of headaches Quinn had no desire to deal with. So, she'd continue to pretend she liked Lauren, and if Grace's track record was any indication, they wouldn't be together for very long anyway. But on the off chance this really was *it* for Grace, Quinn didn't want her dislike of a permanent girlfriend to put a strain on their friendship.

Grace tilted her head to one side and studied Quinn, which made Quinn decidedly uncomfortable. Quinn grabbed a towel and began wiping off the bar as a way to keep from fidgeting under Grace's scrutiny. She hated when Grace did this. It was almost as though she could read Quinn's mind. It seemed there was never anything she could keep secret from Grace.

"Why don't you like her?" Grace finally asked.

"Who?" Quinn thought she sounded convincing, but when Grace rolled her eyes and took a sip of her wine, Quinn knew she wasn't buying the innocent act. She tucked one corner of the towel into the back pocket of her jeans and leaned on the counter again. She stared into Grace's pale blue eyes and shook her head. "How do you do that? It's like you always know what I'm thinking."

"You do the same thing to me, you know," Grace said as she slowly ran a finger around the rim of her wineglass.

"Maybe we've known each other too long," Quinn said with a wink.

"Twenty years is too long? It's not even half of our lives."

Quinn winced as she straightened her posture. She didn't like being reminded she was in her forties. In her mind, she didn't feel any different than she had when she was twenty-five. Her mother liked to point out she didn't act any different now than she had back then either. She turned to enter Grace's glass of wine into the computer before facing her once more.

"Don't think by changing the subject you can get away with not answering my question," Grace said, waving a finger in her face. "Why don't you like her?"

"I'm not going to get into this with you," Quinn told her. She was uneasy with this line of questioning. "I say something bad about her, then you end up marrying her and our friendship is down the drain. It isn't worth the risk."

"I think our friendship is plenty strong enough to withstand brutal honesty when it comes to something so serious, don't you?" Grace reached across the bar and grasped Quinn's wrist, but never broke eye contact. "Imagine how things might have turned out differently if I'd told you about my reservations concerning Juliet. I kept quiet for the same reasons, and you ended up with your heart broken."

"But you were there to pick up the pieces." Quinn hated thinking about her breakup with Juliet. It made her angry, and it made her feel like a fool because she'd chosen to put her trust in a woman who hadn't deserved it. She really hated being made a fool of.

"I was," Grace said. "Just as I know you'll always be there for me, no matter where either of us may end up."

Quinn narrowed her eyes at her, wondering what those words really meant. The tightness in her chest at the thought of Grace possibly moving away was a bit alarming. Maybe too alarming when talking about a friend. Friends didn't always live in close proximity, did they? They had lives, and moved on, and you could talk on the phone a couple times a year and have it seem like no time at all had passed since the last time you saw each other. The thought didn't make the anxiety fade, but actually made it worse. She and Grace hadn't gone more than a couple of days in a row without at least talking on the phone in the two decades they'd been friends.

"Are you trying to tell me something? Are you moving away with her?"

Grace bit her bottom lip the way she always did when she was dreading telling someone something they weren't going to want to hear. Quinn shook her head and pulled her arm away from Grace's grasp.

"There's nothing definite, Quinn," Grace told her. "She's accepted a position at a hospital in Syracuse. She isn't moving until the fall, and who knows what might happen in the meantime? The way my relationships usually go, we might not even still be together by then."

Quinn didn't know what to say. Grace was right about past relationships not working out. Usually after three or four months, it all fizzled out, and Grace was single again. Quinn couldn't understand it, though. Grace was beautiful with her auburn hair and blue eyes. She worked out a couple of times a week so she was in good shape. Why couldn't she make a relationship last?

"Well, if that's the case, then the good doctor is an idiot, and you're better off without her," Quinn finally said. She was relieved when Grace laughed at the remark instead of taking it too seriously. Quinn held up a finger in the direction of the guy at the other end of the bar who was trying to get her attention. "I've got to get back to work."

"Can we talk later? When you're done working?" Grace asked. Quinn nodded. "I'll bring the pizza."

"You certainly know how to get to me, don't you?"

"Of course I do," Grace answered with a smug smile. "I probably know you better than you know yourself."

Of that, Quinn had no doubt.

CHAPTER TWO

Grace watched Quinn as she took care of her customers. She'd been tending bar for so long, she didn't even have to think about what she was doing, which was evident in the way she continued to talk and laugh with the people waiting for their cocktails as she poured the drinks.

She envied the ease with which Quinn dealt with people. It was obviously second nature to her. Grace had to work at interacting with people, which was crazy since she owned her own bookstore. She'd often thought if she could simply own it and do absolutely nothing but deal with the books, she'd be perfectly content. Which, of course, would never work in a retail business.

She had just watched Quinn disappear into the storeroom behind the bar when she was grabbed from behind. She jumped but didn't make a sound as she turned and saw Callie Burke, sexy smile firmly in place on her lips. Quinn's younger sister took after her in the looks and charm department, there was certainly no doubt about that. Grace stood and gave Callie a warm hug and a kiss on her cheek.

"Where's my sister hiding?" Callie asked, glancing around. There was nowhere to sit at the bar, so she stood behind Grace, one hand resting on her shoulder.

"I think she had to change a keg or something," Grace

told her. "What are you doing here? Quinn didn't tell me you were in town."

"Yeah, well, she doesn't know yet," Callie answered with a shrug.

Grace turned in her seat to get a better look at Callie and saw the determined set of her jaw. The muscles there clenched rapidly, a trait she and Quinn shared when something was upsetting them. Callie was still scanning the area behind the bar and refused to meet Grace's eyes.

"What's wrong?" Grace asked, knowing she wouldn't tell her, but feeling like she had to ask. She cared about Callie, but Callie was even more guarded with her emotions than Quinn was. If that were at all possible.

"Nothing," she said, plastering the megawatt, but so obviously fake, smile on her face again. "I just need a drink. It was a long drive from Atlanta."

Just as the gentleman next to Grace vacated his seat, Quinn emerged from behind the bar and gave her little sister a bear hug before Callie even had the chance to grab the now empty bar stool. Grace smiled as she watched the two of them together. She struggled with the lump in her throat at the sibling love, something she'd never experience again since her brother had been killed in Afghanistan six years ago.

"What the hell are you doing here?" Quinn asked, a huge grin on her face. "Why didn't you tell me you were coming for a visit?"

"It's not a visit," Callie told her, and Grace winced at what she suspected was coming.

"Yeah?" Quinn slapped Callie on the back before Grace saw her looking around the immediate vicinity for Callie's girlfriend. "Where's Jan? You didn't make her wait out in the car, did you?"

Callie looked away before mumbling something and

heading for the restroom. Grace hit Quinn in the stomach with the back of her hand. Quinn looked hurt and raised her hands in a gesture of *what the hell was that for?*

"They broke up," Grace said.

"She told you that?" Quinn asked, sounding skeptical. She glanced in the direction Callie had gone. "Why wouldn't she have said something to me?"

"No, she didn't tell me. She didn't have to."

"Then how do you know?"

"Oh, my God, Quinn, the two of you are so much alike it's scary sometimes." Grace shook her head and finished the last of her wine. "You never question it when I know what's going on with you. You both have the same tells. Call me if you need to spend time with her after you get off. Otherwise I'll meet you at your place."

"Don't forget the pizza," Quinn said with a grin.

❖

Grace went home to her apartment, a little one-bedroom above the bookstore she owned. She looked at her cell phone to make sure Lauren hadn't called before plugging it in to charge the battery. She sighed as she collapsed onto the couch. She wasn't entirely sure she was going to move with Lauren, and honestly, Grace wasn't totally convinced Lauren had been serious when she made the suggestion.

"We've just met," Grace said when Lauren told her about the job offer.

"You could come with me," Lauren answered with a shrug.

That was it. Nothing else was said again by either one of them about it. Had she meant it, or was it just something to say, knowing Grace would likely never take her up on the offer?

She'd never intended mentioning it to Quinn, but when she'd asked, Grace couldn't lie to her. Their friendship was so strong though, and she knew Quinn would support her in whatever decision she ultimately made. They'd been best friends since the time they were both working in the same grocery store twenty years ago. It had been awkward between them at first because Quinn expressed an interest in her. Grace admitted to herself she was attracted too, but she'd grown up a loner, and she really wanted a friend more than a lover when they'd met. Quinn agreed to a platonic relationship and never mentioned wanting anything more since.

Grace couldn't say she wasn't disappointed by it, but they'd forged a strong friendship, and they'd seen each other through some pretty rough times. Quinn was always there for her, and she knew by the end of the night Quinn would either have talked her out of going or would be encouraging her to follow her heart.

Grace just wasn't sure which option she was rooting for.

She took a quick shower and headed out to Quinn's.

❖

"How long are you in town for?" Quinn asked Callie as she came around from behind the bar and took a seat next to her. It was almost midnight, and Taylor was taking over until closing as she usually did so Quinn could have something that somewhat resembled a normal life.

"I'm not sure," Callie answered with a shrug.

Quinn didn't miss the fact Chelsea had been making eye contact with Callie for the past hour or so, and Callie didn't seem to be discouraging the attention. She threw an arm around Callie's shoulders and forced her to turn back toward the bar.

"What the fuck?" Callie asked.

"She's too young for you."

"Which is Quinn-speak for back off, I'm interested," Callie said with a knowing grin. "I get it. Message received."

"And here I thought it was Quinn-speak for *you have a girlfriend, Callie*." Quinn felt Callie's shoulders stiffen under her arm, and she wished she'd listened to Grace earlier. It was becoming painfully clear she'd been right about her and Jan breaking up. "You want to talk about it?"

"No." Callie gave a quick shake of her head and downed the rest of the beer she'd been drinking, which was about half a pint. She set it down on the bar a little too hard, causing Taylor to shoot a questioning glance their way.

Quinn waved her off before she could head in their direction. She leaned closer to Callie so she wouldn't have to speak loud enough for anyone else to hear. "That's fine. We don't have to talk right now, but answer me this. Are you all right?"

Callie seemed to struggle with a response, but Quinn waited patiently for an answer. After a few minutes of Callie looking like she was going to say something before other things grabbed her attention, she finally sighed.

"We broke up. If you'd asked me yesterday afternoon if I was all right, I'd have said no." She paused and gave Taylor a nod of appreciation when she set a fresh pint in front of her. Quinn watched Callie watching Taylor as she walked away.

"But?" Quinn prompted her, causing Callie's head to whip around and look at her. "Now you are? All right, I mean."

"Yeah, I think I am," she answered, looking a little surprised. "Being here, seeing you and Grace, and Mom, and being a day removed from what happened, I think I'm just fine. Do you think that's a little fucked up? I mean, I should be upset, shouldn't I?"

"That's something only you can answer," Quinn said. This

was something akin to her situation with Grace. If she said something against Jan, and then they ended up reconciling, she could see things going seriously bad between them. It wasn't something she wanted to happen, so once again she kept her mouth shut.

Callie nodded and glanced over her shoulder toward Chelsea once again before shaking her head and laughing at herself.

"Yeah, I think I'll be fine."

"You need a place to stay tonight?" Quinn asked the question as a common courtesy but held her breath, hoping Callie would say no. She loved her sister dearly, but that didn't mean she wanted to coexist under the same roof with her. She started to panic when Callie hesitated before answering.

"Mom's letting me sleep on her couch tonight," Callie finally said. "Thank you though. You're coming for brunch tomorrow, right?"

"I always do," Quinn said as she stood and pulled her jacket on. "You're sure you don't want to talk about it?"

"Not tonight."

"Okay then." Quinn grasped her shoulder and gave it a quick squeeze. "I'll see you tomorrow."

CHAPTER THREE

"Honey, I'm home," Quinn called out as she walked through the front door of her house.

Grace smiled at the familiar greeting. Quinn said it whenever Grace was there before she got home. She handed a glass filled with bourbon to Quinn and raised her own. "To friendship."

Quinn was looking at her with one eyebrow raised, but she set her glass down. Grace sighed and set hers next to it on the counter.

"You don't usually drink anything stronger than wine," Quinn said, her tone full of concern.

"How's Callie?" A blatant attempt at deflection, but Quinn seemed to go with it.

"They broke up, but she says she's okay," Quinn answered. She walked out to the living room and sat in her usual spot at the end of the couch. Grace took the seat next to her. "She's staying with Mom tonight and said she'd see me tomorrow for brunch. You're coming, right?"

"I can't," Grace said. The disappointed frown Quinn gave her made her almost change her mind. Brunch was a weekly thing, and had been for years, and Grace rarely missed it. She loved Quinn's mother like she was her own.

Grace's parents were killed in a car accident when Grace had been only twelve. Her brother was fourteen at the time, and their grandparents had taken them in without hesitation. They were in their eighties now, and Grace liked to try to spend as much time with them as she could. Especially if she might be moving to Syracuse.

"You're going to the lake?"

Grace nodded. Her grandparents had bought a home on the shore of Lake Erie a few years earlier, and Grace tried to visit them at least once a month. It was a three-hour drive for her now, but from Syracuse it would be almost five. She placed a hand on Quinn's thigh and felt her tense before pulling her hand back.

"This isn't what we were going to talk about."

"No, it isn't." Quinn looked uncomfortable, but she smiled. "You're really going to move to Syracuse?"

"I said I was thinking about it. Lauren won't be moving until the end of October, so we'll have time to figure things out."

"I don't think you should go."

Grace studied Quinn's face. She was so beautiful with her sculpted cheekbones and firm jaw. Her eyes were an amazing shade of green Grace had never seen before. She was wearing her dark brown hair longer these days. It was almost down to her shoulders. When they were younger, she'd often had it cut so short it would spike. Grace noticed a few gray hairs showing, but thought it better to not mention it.

"Why do you think I shouldn't go?"

"Well, there's your bookstore," Quinn said, holding up a finger with each point she made. "And you'd be farther away from your grandparents. You grew up here. And you'd miss me."

Grace smiled at the grin Quinn gave her, coupled with the

nudge of an elbow into her ribs. All of Quinn's points were valid, and it certainly wasn't as if she hadn't thought about all of those things on her own. Grace wasn't getting any younger though, and she was feeling the need to settle down. Ms. Right had proved to be elusive, and Grace finally decided she needed to lower her standards a little.

"All very compelling points," Grace said. "But like I told you, she won't be going for a few more months, so there's time to figure it all out. And I'm not entirely sure I am going. I'm just thinking about it."

Quinn nodded, but she looked far from convinced.

"But the biggest reason I don't think you should go? I don't want you to," Quinn said, her voice quiet. She refused to meet Grace's eyes, and for some reason that bothered Grace.

"Hey," Grace said, placing a hand on Quinn's thigh. "It's not like I'd be going to the end of the earth. Syracuse is only two hours away."

"We've never lived more than ten miles apart since we met. You're my best friend. I've grown rather fond of you." Quinn did look at her then, and the mischievous look in her eye told Grace she was teasing, but Grace knew the statement was rooted in truth.

Quinn rarely shared her real feelings without the cloak of humor. Grace had to admit she'd come by the trait honestly, because her mother, Linda, was the same way. Callie too. Grace wasn't familiar enough with Beth and Meg, Quinn's older sisters, to know if they were the same way. She was willing to bet, given the animosity between the two older and two younger Burke sisters, the two sets of siblings probably had absolutely nothing in common.

"I've grown rather fond of you too," Grace said with a smile. Quinn rested her head on the back of the couch and stared at the ceiling. Grace reached for her hand, and Quinn jumped slightly at the touch but didn't pull away. "I shouldn't have even said anything about it until I knew for sure what I was going to do."

"No, you shouldn't have," Quinn said. She closed her eyes and reveled in the warmth of the hand covering hers. She turned her hand over so they could lace their fingers together, an innocuous motion she'd done countless times in the past, but this time she had to bite her tongue to keep from saying something she might regret. Instead, she put on a fake smile she hoped Grace wouldn't see right through and met her eyes. "I'm sorry. I'm just in a weird mood tonight. The bar's closing for a couple of months for renovations soon, and then you hit me with this news. You know I'll support you in whatever you choose to do, right? I really only want you to be happy."

"I do know that," Grace answered with a nod. "But for some reason you don't think Lauren is the one who'll make me happy. Why is that?"

Quinn stared at her, not knowing how in the hell to answer the question. After a moment, she squeezed Grace's hand gently and decided to take a stab at it.

"Honestly? I don't even know her, so I can't possibly know that about her. In fact, if you were to bring her in here along with four random women, I wouldn't even be able to pick her out of the group. That's how much I dismissed her as suitable relationship material for you. She's not your type."

"I don't have a type." Grace pulled her hand away and got up to start pacing. Quinn smiled to herself because it was what Grace always did when she was agitated about something. And she was damn cute when she was agitated.

"You do."

"Okay, smart-ass, what's my type?" Grace stopped pacing and pinned Quinn to the couch with her stare.

"She's a doctor. That's so not your type. Remember Holly?"

Grace let out an exasperated sigh and placed her hands on her hips. Maybe reminding her of the woman who had used the excuse of being on call in order to cheat on her hadn't been the wisest choice, but it was too late now.

"I didn't ask you what *isn't* my type. I asked you what is."

"I don't want to do this, okay?" Quinn shook her head. This night was going nothing like she'd hoped, but that had started the moment Grace mentioned the possibility of moving to Syracuse. "I have zero interest in arguing with you. I should have kept my mouth shut and just said I'm happy for you."

"Can we just start the evening over again?" Grace asked. She flopped onto the couch next to Quinn again, wrapping her arms around Quinn and laying her head on her shoulder. "Pretend I never said anything about Syracuse?"

"We can try," Quinn managed to say in spite of the tightness in her throat. Grace felt so good leaning against her she was experiencing sensory overload. She tried to regulate her breathing so Grace wouldn't have any idea of the things racing through her mind. She turned her head slightly and took in the scent of Grace's aloe and shea butter shampoo.

She sighed when she tried to pull away, but Grace held on tight to her arm. They were friends. She shouldn't be having romantic feelings for her, but it was what always happened when Grace was getting serious about someone. And possibly moving two hours away definitely fell under the category of serious. She'd never told Grace about these feelings, because she knew they always went away, sort of, once Grace was single again, so why rock the boat, so to speak?

CHAPTER FOUR

W here's Grace this morning?" Quinn's mother asked, hand on hip, as soon as Quinn was in the door.

"She drove to the lake to see her grandparents today," Callie answered as she came down the hall, her hair still wet from a shower. Quinn looked at her in disbelief and Callie simply shrugged. They walked into the kitchen, and Callie snagged a biscuit on her way past the table. Their mother slapped her on the arm.

"Put that down. It's for breakfast."

"Yeah? Quinn's here. Who else are you waiting for?"

"No one, but that isn't the point," their mother answered. Quinn couldn't hide the smirk, and she sidestepped the elbow Callie threw her way.

"Fine."

"How did you know she was going to her grandparents' today?" Quinn couldn't hold back her curiosity any longer.

"She called me last night to make sure I was all right." Callie handed her a cup of coffee, and they both sat at the table. "She usually comes to breakfast every Sunday, doesn't she?"

"Usually, yeah," Quinn said before taking a sip.

"What did you do to piss her off?" Callie grinned, her eyes peeking over her cup and showing her amusement.

"Fuck you," Quinn said quietly so their mother wouldn't hear. Callie laughed, and Quinn couldn't help but join her. Callie's laugh was infectious. It always had been.

"Have you talked to Quinn yet?" their mother asked from the stove, her back to them.

Quinn raised an eyebrow in question, but Callie avoided her gaze. Quinn placed her cup on the table in front of her and ran a hand through her hair before leaning against the back of her chair.

"Talked to me about what?"

"Jan and I broke up," Callie finally said after a few seconds of fidgeting. "But you already know that, yeah?"

Quinn waited, knowing Callie needed time to gather her thoughts. She was pretty sure she knew where this was headed, and it didn't make her very happy. Quinn liked living by herself. It was peaceful. Tranquil, even, and she knew it would be anything but if Callie moved in.

"I was hoping I could stay with you for a bit."

"Why can't you stay here?" Quinn asked.

"Because I'm old, and I've earned the right to my privacy," her mother said as she set plates full of food in front of them both.

"I haven't earned the right to my privacy?" Quinn asked, not at all liking that she was being backed into a corner.

"What if I had a gentleman stay over," their mother said with a wicked grin, "and he wanted to chase me through the apartment naked?"

"Oh, Jesus, Mom," Quinn said as she shook her head and put her hands up. "I'm never going to get that visual out of my head."

"I would say if he's chasing you through the apartment naked, then chances are he's no gentleman," Callie said before picking up a slice of bacon and shoving it in her mouth.

Their mother chuckled as she turned and headed back for more plates. Quinn took the opportunity to give her little sister a kick in the shin.

"Ow!" Callie said with a grimace as she reached down to rub her leg. "What the hell was that for?"

"It doesn't bother you to think about her having sex?" Quinn kept her voice down and leaned forward.

"Trust me, I *don't* think about her having sex. But I hope to God I'm still having sex when I'm her age." Callie laughed at what Quinn knew was her shocked expression.

"She's our mother."

"I'm well aware of that." Callie took another bite of bacon and looked thoughtful as she chewed. "But she's also human, and all humans are sexual beings."

Quinn decided to let it go when their mother joined them at the table. She was about to start eating when she remembered what had brought them to the subject in the first place.

"So, you're moving back up here?" Quinn watched as a flicker of sadness flashed through Callie's eyes. She didn't want to pry, but she also knew it would likely be the only way to get the entire story out of her. "What exactly happened?"

Callie looked her in the eye, but didn't answer right away. Quinn glanced at her mother, but she was busy shoveling food in her mouth and acting as if she weren't listening. Quinn was about to give up waiting and start in on her own breakfast when Callie finally spoke.

"She told me she wasn't in love with me anymore."

"Women suck, don't they?" Quinn said quietly. She'd really thought Callie and Jan would be together forever. Of course, given how her own relationship had ended, Quinn could admit to herself she certainly wasn't the best judge when it came to women, but Jan didn't seem anything like Juliet.

"She swore to me she never slept with anyone else," Callie

said. "But she'd been spending a lot of time with some woman she works with. I've never met her. They went out for drinks a couple days a week after work, and they started bowling together in a league."

"How could you not have known what was happening?" Quinn asked, and she wanted to immediately swallow her words.

"It's not like I was working a nine-to-five, Quinn." Callie leaned against the back of her chair and let out an exasperated sigh. "Murderers don't give a rat's ass what time of day it is. To be honest, I was glad she'd found a friend. Happy she wasn't sitting around all alone every night. It's probably my own fault that we grew apart."

"Did she leave you?" Quinn asked.

"I left," Callie said, jamming her thumb into her chest. "I had the day off and she called me on her lunch hour to tell me she wanted to break up. She made me promise we could talk about it when she got home, but I packed my stuff and was gone within an hour of hanging up with her."

"So you're here to stay," Quinn said, happy to have her back home, but on the other hand dreading she might turn into the houseguest that never leaves.

"I just need a place to stay until I get settled. I have an interview with the Rochester PD on Wednesday."

"You think they'll hire you back?" their mother asked, sounding skeptical.

Quinn knew Callie was a good cop, and she had a lot of friends in Rochester. But she hadn't left on the best of terms, having given only two days' notice before running away to Atlanta because Jan had been transferred.

"I'm hoping they will," Callie answered. "I talked to Amanda Rodgers on Friday. In fact, she's the one who got me the interview."

"She was your sergeant, right?" Quinn asked, trying to remember.

"Yeah, but she's a lieutenant now. She's in charge of homicide. I told her everything that happened, and she seems happy at the prospect of getting me back there."

Quinn didn't say anything. She wasn't sure she wanted to give up her privacy, but she had a spare bedroom and her mother didn't. Having Callie there would throw a monkey wrench in her private life, but she supposed she could deal with just hanging out with her sister for a few weeks. Besides, the bar was closed soon for renovations, so it wouldn't be as easy to meet new women.

"You can stay with me, but no more than two months."

"It won't be nearly that long if I get my old job back," Callie said, obviously happy to have at least one problem in her life solved.

"You'll have to go to bingo with us tomorrow night," their mother said. "You'll have fun. Maybe you can meet someone there."

Quinn stifled a laugh. She took her mother to bingo every week, and in the past three years, she'd noticed there weren't any regulars there under the age of retirement. Somehow Quinn couldn't quite see her thirty-nine-year-old sister hooking up with a senior citizen.

❖

"Thank you again for letting me stay here," Callie said when Quinn showed her to the bedroom she'd be staying in. "I'll stay out of your way. If you want to bring someone home, just let me know, and I'll find somewhere else to be."

"If it happens, I'll go to her place, so don't worry about it," Quinn said. She wasn't going to admit she didn't really want to be with anyone lately. Callie had been trying to get her to acknowledge her feelings for Grace for years. All because Quinn had gotten a little pissy when Callie dated Grace a few times fifteen years ago. "You do the same. Just text me if you want me to give you some privacy."

"Won't be an issue," Callie said with a chuckle and a shake of her head.

"Why not? You were quite the player before you met Jan."

"I spent a lot of time alone in the car on the way up here, and I came to realize I kind of like my own company. I think I want to just be by myself for a bit, and not complicate things with women, you know what I mean?"

"Unless of course you meet someone irresistible," Quinn said.

"Well, yeah," Callie answered with a grin. "I would think that goes without saying."

Quinn nodded before looking at her watch. Grace usually called her when she arrived at her grandparents' house, and she should have been there an hour ago if she'd left at the time she planned to.

"I'm going to let you get settled in," she said as she pushed off the doorjamb. "I'll be downstairs."

Quinn went to the kitchen for a glass of water before settling in on the couch and pulling her phone out. No missed calls. She couldn't figure out why Grace hadn't called, or even texted. She closed her eyes and rested her head on the back of the couch, the phone still held in her hand.

She thought about Grace. She couldn't help it. If she was being honest with herself, she could admit she'd probably been falling in love with Grace a little bit at a time over the past twenty years. Never enough to have it slap her in the face, but enough for it to have disrupted life on some level. On that same level, she knew it was the reason she didn't like Lauren.

Having these kinds of feelings about her best friend wasn't what she wanted. She knew it wasn't what Grace wanted. Grace made it clear when they first met that she was interested in a friend, not looking for a *girl*friend. She wasn't too proud to admit to herself Grace had bruised her still developing ego, but back then Quinn didn't have too many people she could call friends either, so it worked out for both of them.

Until now.

Quinn could kid herself about not knowing where these feelings came from, just as they always did when Grace started dating someone new. But she did know. She was in love with Grace, and she was afraid about what it might mean. On the one hand, it felt so very wrong because they were best friends. But on the other hand, it felt so very *right*. It felt more right than it had ever felt with Juliet, and the thought scared the hell out of Quinn.

For the longest time, Grace had been the player. She was well-known at all the hippest clubs, and never spent more than one or two nights with the same woman. Quinn, on the other hand, wanted someone to settle down with. To grow old with. She spent years living vicariously through Grace. Quinn thought she'd found what she'd been searching for in Juliet. Boy, had she been wrong.

After three years together, Juliet came home from work one night and announced she was leaving. She'd fallen in love with someone else. Someone younger. Quinn pleaded with her to reconsider, but it did no good. Juliet had blamed all their problems on Quinn, saying she'd always thought Quinn had been in love with Grace, an accusation Quinn denied profusely. Maybe a little too profusely.

The next day, when Quinn went into the bank to deposit her paycheck, she was hit with the harsh reality of her situation. Juliet had withdrawn all but ten dollars from their joint account.

There had been over five thousand in the account just a few days earlier. The vast majority of it was Quinn's, money she'd been putting away for their future.

In that moment, Quinn really didn't give a flying fuck if Juliet ever came back. Quinn suddenly became the player Grace had always been, but now Grace was looking to settle down. That was eighteen months ago, and Quinn was ready now. Ready to put her heart on the line once again, but now Lauren was in the picture.

She decided she just needed to give herself time. These feelings for Grace would diminish, just as they always had in the past, right? She sighed as she resigned herself to being happy for Grace if she truly had found her Ms. Right. Unfortunately, that didn't stop the smile or the uptick in her pulse rate when her phone rang and she saw Grace's name on the display.

CHAPTER FIVE

I was beginning to worry you'd been in an accident or something," Quinn said when she answered the phone.

"I'm so sorry I didn't call earlier," Grace told her, her voice quiet so as not to disturb her grandparents watching the Pittsburgh Pirates baseball game in the other room. "Gran had me working in the garden with her the moment I got out of the car."

"I'm just glad you made it there okay."

"You worry too much." Grace smiled, knowing Quinn couldn't possibly change it about herself. And Grace found it comforting to know she cared so much.

"Mom asked about you this morning. She wanted me to be sure and remind you about bingo tomorrow night."

"I wouldn't miss it," Grace said. "It's surprisingly fun. More than I thought it would be in the beginning."

"It probably helps that you have more luck at it than anyone else in the joint." Quinn chuckled. "Callie's going too. And she's staying with me until she gets back on her feet because you were right. She left Jan. She said you called her last night after you left my place."

"I thought she might need to talk." Grace stepped out to

the back deck that overlooked Lake Erie. It was hot outside, spring finally stepping aside so summer could take over unimpeded, but her grandparents kept the house so cold it was almost a welcome relief. She leaned one hip against the railing and watched them through the window. "Is she okay?"

"I think so," Quinn said, sounding a little apprehensive. "At least she says she is."

Grace didn't believe it. Callie and Quinn were both masters at hiding their emotions, and she found it funny, in a strange way, that neither of them could read each other. Callie was still in high school the first time Grace met her, but Grace knew even then that she was exactly like Quinn. Which meant Callie was probably just as devastated now as Quinn had been when her relationship ended. They weren't the types to give their hearts easily, so when they did it was with the understanding it was for the long haul.

"I should probably go because it's almost time for the seventh inning stretch, which means I need to have lunch ready for them." Grace smiled when she heard Quinn laugh. When she was a kid, she and her brother had to have lunch ready at the middle of the seventh inning. Grace wasn't at their house very often for baseball now, but when she was, it was something she still did for them. Only now she did it because it was comforting, not because it was something she had to do.

"All right. Come by tonight if you don't get home too late."

"I will. Good-bye."

Grace hit the disconnect button but didn't move to go into the house right away. She wondered why it was Quinn was always checking up on her, but none of the women she'd been involved with did. Take Lauren for instance. They had plans for dinner on Wednesday, but Grace knew she wouldn't talk to her before then, and that was okay. She knew Lauren wasn't the type to call just for a chat. But if she went an entire day without at least talking to Quinn on the phone, everything felt off-kilter.

Not wanting to dwell on it too much, she went inside to make a couple of cans of soup and some grilled cheese sandwiches for her grandparents and herself.

❖

"How is Quinn doing, dear?" her grandmother asked when they were finished with lunch and the seventh inning was over.

"She's fine. Why do you ask?" Grace said, feeling her grandfather's eyes on her as well.

"You just don't bring her around much anymore," he said.

"I usually took your grandfather with me whenever I'd go to visit family."

Grace shook her head. They'd had this conversation many times before. She wasn't sure if they were that forgetful, or if they simply really liked Quinn and wished they were a couple.

"You know Quinn and I aren't involved. We're friends. We've always been just friends."

Her grandmother clicked her tongue and stood to take the dirty dishes to the kitchen. Her grandfather was watching the game again, so Grace stood to follow her.

"Gram, you do know we aren't involved, right?"

"I'm not senile," she answered with a shake of her head. She ran the plates and bowls under water before turning to look at Grace. "We both know you're just friends."

"Then why do you keep asking me things like that?"

"I've seen the way you two look at each other. Your grandfather and I have both seen it. It's the way he used to look at me. Like I was the most beautiful woman in the world."

"You're crazy, Gram," Grace said, wondering how on earth they could think that. Or even why they spent time discussing her love life. She was pretty sure she'd never looked at Quinn that way and was almost positive Quinn had never looked at her that way. Grace imagined that would be the kind of look you couldn't easily forget.

"We may be older than dirt," her grandfather said from behind her, causing Grace to jump and let out a shout at the surprise of finding him there, "but I can assure you neither of us is crazy. We may forget from time to time where we put the remote for the television, but that doesn't make us senile either."

"Grandpa—"

"And I have a bone to pick with you, old woman," he said, walking past Grace and taking her grandmother's hands in his. "I *still* look at you that way, because you *are* the most beautiful woman in the world."

Grace retreated to the living room when her grandmother slid her arms around his neck and kissed him. She hoped someday she would find the kind of love they shared. She chuckled to herself at the thought of Quinn looking at her that way. Yes, Quinn had shown an interest in her when they'd first met, but once Grace told her she'd only wanted a friend, things turned strictly platonic and had been that way ever since. It was ludicrous to even think about.

❖

"Bingo!" Grace yelled just eight numbers into the third game. There was a collective groan from the more than one hundred people seated in the fire hall. Quinn set her dauber down on the table a little too hard and glared at her from directly across the table. Grace shrugged as she handed the card to one of the checkers for verification. "What?"

"How the hell are you so lucky at this?" Quinn asked.

"It's not luck," Grace answered, unable to keep the smirk off her face. "It's skill."

"Skill, my ass." Quinn sighed and ran a hand through her hair.

"Thank you," Grace said to the woman who handed her the money. She shoved the cash into the pocket of her jeans and readied herself for the next game. She gave Quinn what she hoped was an innocent smile. "You've won before."

"Once, and that was like a year ago. You've won about thirty times since then."

"Jealous much?" Callie asked with an elbow to Quinn's side. Quinn retaliated with a hard jab to Callie's upper arm. Callie hissed in pain as she covered the area with a hand. "What the hell is wrong with you?"

"Knock it off, both of you," their mother said in a loud whisper. "I swear it's like you're twelve and nine all over again."

They were all quiet then, until Grace's cell phone began to ring. Loudly. She fumbled in the pocket of her cargo shorts for what seemed like an eternity while people around them grumbled in irritation. Never mess with old people and their bingo night, she thought as she finally got hold of the phone and pulled it out. She silenced the ringer and placed the phone on the table. It was Lauren, and although Grace was curious as to why she'd call when they were meeting for dinner in two nights, she wasn't about to have a phone conversation in the middle of a bingo game. These people would probably string her up if she did. She'd just call her back later.

"Who was that?" Callie asked casually once a woman a few tables away called bingo.

"Grace's new girlfriend," Quinn answered, sounding a bit moody. Of course she would have seen the letter "L" on the display and knew it was Lauren.

"What?" Callie and their mother asked in unison.

"My girlfriend," Grace repeated for them.

"Why am I just hearing about this now?" Callie asked.

"Why do you care?" Quinn asked as she straightened her cards for the next game.

"Why do you sound so pissy?"

"Quinn thinks she isn't my type." Grace threw it out there, knowing Callie would set Quinn straight on that misguided opinion.

"Then she probably isn't," Callie said, her tone indicating the matter was settled.

Grace looked back and forth between Quinn and Callie, and the grin on Quinn's face pushed her over the edge.

"What the fuck?" she asked, apparently louder than she'd meant to if the shocked sounds from the people around them were any indication. She glanced around and offered apologies before turning her anger back to Callie, her voice more hushed this time. "You haven't even met her, so how could you possibly agree?"

Callie glanced at Quinn, who was obviously trying her best to let them think she was ignoring the conversation, before shrugging and smiling as her attention turned back to Grace.

"Is she anything at all like Quinn?"

What? Grace felt her jaw drop, and she wondered why the question was even asked. What in the hell did Quinn have to do with it? To her credit, Quinn seemed as surprised by the question as Grace.

"No," Grace finally answered.

"Well then, there's your answer. She's definitely not your type." Callie lowered her gaze to the bingo cards on the table in front of her and tried to catch up.

"What the hell is that supposed to mean?" Quinn asked.

"You know exactly what she means, and the three of you need to shut up," their mother said. "Some of us are trying to concentrate here."

Quinn looked as though she wanted to say something else, but must have thought better of it because none of them said another word about it for the rest of the evening.

CHAPTER SIX

W hat are you going to be doing while the bar is closed for a month?" Taylor asked.

Quinn sat across the desk from her as Taylor was entering information into her computer. This was their weekly employee meeting, and the rest of the crew had been dismissed. Quinn glanced at her watch. She hated being cooped up in an office. It was Saturday night, and the last day they would be open before renovations on the bar began. She'd come in early to try to get the bar stocked, not to spend twice as long as usual in the office for their meeting.

"Why?" Quinn couldn't help the grin she felt forming. "Afraid I'll jump ship for a more lucrative gig?"

Taylor leaned back in her chair and removed her reading glasses as she regarded Quinn for a moment. Quinn felt a little uncomfortable at being studied so openly.

"Always," Taylor said after a few moments. She set her glasses on the desk and rubbed her eyes. "You're a popular bartender, and I know you're pretty well-known here in Brockport, and in Rochester too."

"I'm not going anywhere, Taylor, you know that," Quinn said with a shake of her head. "You're like family to me, and honestly? I don't think I could work for anyone else after being with you for so long."

"Then what are you going to do?"

"I'll be helping Grace out at the bookstore. She's been putting off hiring a full-time employee, and my lending a hand will help her delay it until the kids come back to school next fall."

"You're a good friend," Taylor said with a nod. "Will she be paying you?"

"Yeah," Quinn said, even though Grace wasn't. She was doing it simply to help her out. Quinn studied Taylor and noticed she looked tired. Worn out even. Her partner of twelve years had been a firefighter, and she'd died on the job a little over two years ago. No, it was almost three years ago exactly, Quinn realized after doing a little quick math in her head. Damn, where had the time gone? Most days it didn't seem to affect Taylor like it had in the beginning, but the anniversary had to be hard on her. "Are you okay?"

"I'm fine," Taylor said quickly. "Just tired is all. I haven't been sleeping well lately."

"You know you can call me if you ever need to talk, right?"

"Thank you." Taylor looked as though she wanted to say something, so Quinn waited her out. "I think I want to start spending less time here. It seems like I'm stuck in this office for days on end sometimes. I think I need to start living my life again."

"Have you met someone?" Quinn asked, wondering if there might be a different reason for Taylor's tiredness than she'd originally thought.

"No," Taylor answered with a laugh. "I don't know if I ever will, but Andrea and I always wanted to travel. I think I might go on a cruise or something. Of course, I may find I can't handle being away from the bar for very long, but I want to give it a try."

"Good for you," Taylor said. "I think Andrea would be happy about that."

"Me too." Taylor smiled at her and put her glasses back on. "Of course, that would mean I'd need to find someone to take care of things here."

Quinn shook her head. They'd had this conversation too many times. She enjoyed tending bar but had no desire to spend half of her shift or more stuck in an office doing paperwork. She'd seen the stress Taylor was under most of the time. Being the head bartender in a bar that only employed two other people was perfect for Quinn.

"Let me know when you find someone for the job," Quinn said as she stood and headed for the door. "I'll do what I can to help train them."

"Quinn, would you please think about it?" Taylor pushed away from her desk and walked to her, a folded piece of paper in her hand. She held it out to Quinn, who took it reluctantly. "That's what I can pay you. I trust you, Quinn, and I'm not sure I could find someone else I would like and genuinely feel good about putting in charge of things. Think about it?"

"Yeah, fine," Quinn said. She shoved the paper into the back pocket of her jeans without looking at it. "I will."

"No, you won't." Taylor laughed and went back to her desk. "I know you. You'll either put it on your dresser and it will get buried under other things, or you'll forget about it, and it'll end up going through the wash. Either way, you'll put it out of your mind and won't give it another thought."

"Maybe you don't know me as well as you think you do." Quinn hated the defensive tone in her voice, but she knew Taylor was right in her assessment, and it irked her. "I said I'd think about it, and I will."

"Okay," Taylor said without looking up from the computer screen.

Quinn sighed and left the office, shutting the door behind her. She hadn't made it to the bar before she felt her phone vibrating against her hip. She smiled when she saw Grace's name on the display and swiped the screen to answer the call.

"Why are you calling me when you've got a dinner date with a hot surgeon?"

"She canceled because she had an emergency come in."

Quinn frowned and stopped her forward motion when she saw the doctor in question sitting at the bar. And she wasn't alone. In fact, she seemed to be quite chummy with the woman in the seat next to her.

"Quinn, are you there?" Grace had that annoyed tone in her voice. She didn't like it when Quinn was only half paying attention to their conversation.

"Yeah, I'm sorry," Quinn said in her best fake cheerful voice. "We're getting slammed here tonight. It's the last night we're open, and the college kids are going home next week. I guess this is their last hurrah, so to speak."

"Oh," Grace said, sounding utterly disappointed. "I thought I might come by and see you, but I guess I probably shouldn't if you're that busy."

There was enough background noise to make Quinn's excuse plausible, but she hated lying to Grace. What she hated even more was the fact Grace's girlfriend was in *her* bar with a woman who was definitely not Grace. Even though Quinn knew she would tell Grace about it, she couldn't bring herself to do it over the phone.

"Yeah, probably not a good idea tonight," Quinn told her. She moved closer to a group of students who were laughing about something so Grace would hear them and believe the bar was packed. "You'll be at brunch tomorrow, right?"

"I'll be there," Grace assured her.

"You know what time I'll be home if you need to talk later," Quinn said. "And just think, after tonight, I'll be all yours for a month or so."

Grace said good-bye, sounding more upbeat than she had when their conversation began. Quinn shoved the phone back into its holster on her hip and made her way behind the bar. She stopped in front of Lauren and wiped down the bar with a forced smile. Camille, her other bartender, had obviously already waited on them, but they looked like they needed refills.

"Can I get you ladies another?" she asked.

Lauren didn't answer her, and she didn't even spare so much as a glance in Quinn's direction. She simply waved a hand at her to tell her to get lost. She was obviously focused on her date and didn't want to be disturbed.

Too bad.

"Excuse me," Quinn said, trying to sound surprised. She hoped she was pulling it off. "Lauren, isn't it?"

Quinn smiled her satisfaction, because that got her attention. Lauren's head whipped around so fast Quinn thought she wouldn't be able to stop it without causing injury to herself. It was obvious Lauren was trying to place her, which pissed Quinn off.

"Quinn," she finally said, hoping to jog Lauren's memory. She probably met so many women she couldn't keep them straight. Quinn wondered briefly if Lauren was trying to remember if she'd slept with her. "I'm a friend of Grace's. Speaking of Grace, where is she?"

"Grace?" Lauren asked, at least having the decency to look embarrassed.

"Yeah, she said you two were going out to dinner tonight." Quinn made a point of looking at the woman next to Lauren, who looked as though she were getting to see the whole picture all of a sudden. Quinn hoped she wasn't ruining Lauren's evening, but no. Not really. She hoped she was ruining Lauren's day. Month. *Year* even.

"We broke up," Lauren said quickly as she put a hand on her date's arm to stop her from leaving. "We did. We broke up."

"Maybe I should have reminded you, but Grace is my *best* friend. She would have told me if you broke up." Quinn tried not to smile too smugly, but she was sure she wasn't accomplishing it. She didn't care. She wanted this other woman to know what she was getting involved with.

"Maybe you aren't such besties, and maybe she doesn't tell you everything," Lauren hissed.

"I could call her and clear this up right now," Quinn said. She pulled her phone out and swiped the screen.

"No, we're leaving," Lauren said.

"I'd like to hear it from her that you broke up," her date said, looking at Quinn.

"We're leaving," Lauren told her as she grabbed her hand and pulled her toward the door. Before they got there, Quinn saw Lauren say something to her before turning and heading back toward Quinn. "This isn't what it looks like."

"Really?" Quinn asked. "Not much else it could be if you wanted her to believe you were single. Plus the fact I just got off the phone with Grace, who told me you canceled your plans because of an emergency at the hospital. So tell me, Lauren, what else could it be?"

"I'm dropping her off and going right home," Lauren assured her. Quinn wasn't buying it. "I want to thank you for keeping me from making a horrible mistake. Promise me you won't say anything to Grace. I swear I'll make this right with her."

Quinn didn't say anything, because what could she possibly say to someone she didn't believe? She watched Lauren as she exited the bar and shook her head, but resisted the urge to call Grace. This wasn't something Quinn could tell her over the phone. This had to be a face-to-face conversation.

CHAPTER SEVEN

Quinn spent the next two days worrying endlessly over whether or not to say anything about Lauren to Grace. She hadn't promised Lauren she'd keep her mouth shut, but she also didn't relish having the conversation with Grace. She did not want to be the one to tell Grace her girlfriend was cheating on her. Of course, if Grace found out on her own, and then discovered Quinn had known about it and not said something, who knew what might happen then?

"You're thinking way too hard," Callie said as she walked into the kitchen Tuesday morning. "I can see the steam coming out your ears."

"Very funny," Quinn muttered before rubbing a hand over her face. This was the first day she was going to be helping Grace at the bookstore, and since they hadn't seen much of each other since bingo over a week ago, Quinn wasn't looking forward to it. Brunch at her mother's had been strained after the events of Saturday night, and she didn't like feeling that way with Grace.

"You want to talk?"

Quinn met Callie's eyes and considered it for a moment. Callie's expression was serious, and Quinn wasn't used to that. Callie was always the jokester. The comedian of the family. Seeing this seriousness directed at her was disconcerting for Quinn.

"No," Quinn said after a moment. "I'm going to be late if I don't get moving."

"If you change your mind, you know where I am," Callie said with a shrug as if it made no difference to her one way or the other. Quinn could tell it did though, and she felt bad for blowing her off. "You may find this hard to believe, but I've become a good listener over the years. And I've been known to give some pretty decent advice from time to time."

"Maybe later," Quinn said. "What are your plans for the day?"

"I'm going to Rochester to meet with some of the muckety-mucks about getting hired back onto the police force," Callie told her. "I thought I'd surprise Mom and take her out to lunch when I'm done."

"She'll like that." Quinn downed the rest of her coffee and took the cup to the sink to rinse it out. She grabbed her keys off the counter and headed for the door. "I'll see you tonight. Good luck in Rochester."

Quinn knew Callie had agonized over how she left the force. She just hoped the people in charge could look past that and judge her simply on her work performance. Callie was a damn good detective, and the Rochester PD would be lucky to have her.

She glanced at the clock in her car and cursed under her breath. Her first day on the job and she was going to be late. It probably wasn't the best way to get things back on track with Grace, but it wasn't like she was getting paid to help her out. What was she going to do, fire her? Actually, she might if Quinn decided to tell her about Lauren. She put it out of her head as she backed out of the driveway and headed toward the bookstore.

❖

Quinn was a little nervous when Grace left her to run the store while she went to get lunch for both of them. Quinn had offered to go instead, but she had the sneaking suspicion Grace was leaving her alone in the store as punishment for arriving a few minutes late that morning. Oh well, how hard could it be? All she had to do was scan a barcode and collect the money if anyone should want to buy something before she got back. She silently prayed no one would come in.

She was tempted to lock the door so no one *could* get in, but she knew Grace wouldn't be happy if she did that. Quinn busied herself with sorting the books they'd received that morning by genre and author so it would be easier to shelve them all once they were finished eating lunch. Her head whipped up at the sound of the bell indicating someone was entering the store. She let out a sigh of relief when she saw Grace, but then her heart sank when Lauren walked in right behind her. She smiled and waved at Grace before grabbing a stack of books and walking away.

"Listen, can we have dinner tomorrow night?" Lauren asked after Quinn disappeared with an armful of books.

"Sure," Grace answered, wondering what was up.

"Good." Lauren seemed relieved, and it made Grace even more curious. "I wanted to talk to you about something."

"Okay." Grace was really wondering now. Lauren hardly ever wanted to talk. She was very guarded about the things she shared. Hey, maybe she really was like Quinn, she thought, making a mental note to shove it in Callie's face. The idea of Lauren being anything like Quinn simultaneously thrilled and scared her. What could it possibly mean in the grand scheme of things? The look on her face must have given her dismay away.

"Hey, are you all right?" Lauren asked with a hand to her arm.

"Fine," Grace said with a quick nod and a smile she hoped wasn't obviously forced. "I'll see you tomorrow night. Should we meet somewhere?"

They ironed out all the details and then Lauren finally left the store. Grace couldn't put a finger on what was bothering her more—Lauren and Quinn having any personal traits in common at all, or the thought that maybe Callie was right. Maybe *Quinn* was her type. It wasn't as though she hadn't considered it before. Hell, Quinn was everybody's type.

There'd been a few times over the course of the years she'd found herself wondering if she and Quinn really should be together. The problem was, their friendship was so tight, she'd never felt comfortable taking the risk. Besides, they'd never seemed to be at the same points in life as far as relationships went. For instance, when Grace finally made the decision she was ready to settle down, Quinn had been with Juliet. Grace had felt so guilty when Juliet broke Quinn's heart because she was so happy it was over. Inwardly, of course. She would never have expressed her joy to Quinn, or anyone else for that matter.

But then Quinn decided Grace had it right all along. Play the field and nobody can break your heart. Grace finally came to her senses and took it for what it was—a simple crush on her best friend. No big deal. Everybody experienced it, right? Grace sighed when she heard someone enter the store. It was no use entertaining the possibility of anything more than friendship with Quinn. It would never work out anyway. They knew each other too well.

"Excuse me," said a woman as she approached the counter. Grace looked up and smiled, but the woman seemed upset about something.

"Can I help you?" Grace asked in the overly cheery voice

she reserved just for the customers she was certain were going to be a problem.

"Yes, I want to return this book," she said. She pulled the book out of her oversized purse and placed it on the counter. Her lips were pressed together and she crossed her arms while she waited.

Grace stared down at the book in disbelief. A quick search of her inventory records confirmed her suspicion. She'd sold her last copy of it almost a year ago and hadn't ordered more because it had sat on the shelf for so long.

"Do you have your receipt?" she asked.

"What?" The woman's arms dropped to her sides and she stared at Grace as though she'd sprouted another head. "No, I don't. I just bought it a couple of weeks ago. You should have it in your records."

Grace took a deep breath but her smile, fake as it was, never wavered. She nodded and turned her attention back to the computer. She could feel Quinn watching from a few feet away. She pretended to do another search before looking back up.

"I'm sorry, but according to the computer, I haven't stocked this book since last summer."

"Your computer must be wrong. Check it again." The woman began drumming her fingers on the counter. Nervous or impatient, Grace wasn't quite sure, but she was betting on nervous. This woman probably thought since she was a small independent store, she must not keep very good records of her inventory.

Grace scanned the ISBN number again only to have the same information come up on the screen. She turned the monitor so the woman could see for herself as she pointed out the details.

"See? This is the date for the last copy we sold. It was last August."

"This is obviously wrong, dear. I want to see your manager."

"I am the manager." Grace fought to keep her tone even. She turned the monitor back to where it was supposed to be and leaned on the counter. Her smile was genuine now, because she knew exactly what was coming next.

"Then I want to talk to the owner." The smirk on the woman's face indicated to Grace that she always got her way. When Grace didn't move right away, she looked over at Quinn, who was walking behind the counter to stand next to Grace. "Are you the owner?"

"No, ma'am," Quinn said with an easy smile. "You're already talking to the owner."

The woman rolled her eyes and looked back to Grace.

"Didn't your parents ever teach you that the customer is always right?"

"Of course they did." Grace opened the cash register and pulled out the money for the woman. Just before handing it to her though, she put the cash back and slammed the drawer shut again. "But actually, what they said was the customer's always right, except when they're not. Don't come back here, because next time, I'll call the police."

"For what?"

"You're trying to steal from me, plain and simple."

The woman muttered something under her breath before shoving the book back in her purse and storming out the front door. Grace was sure she was going to try to return it to other stores as well.

"How do you put up with people like that day in and day out?" Quinn asked when she was finally gone.

"I'd like to say it doesn't happen often, but I'd be lying.

You get used to it." Grace shrugged and went back to what she'd been doing before leaving to get their lunch earlier— entering books they'd received that morning into the computer.

"If you say so." Quinn grabbed another stack and turned to go put them on the shelves. Helping out while the bar was closed for renovations was turning out to be a good thing. It got Quinn out of the house, and free labor meant Grace could go a little while longer without hiring someone new. Well, her labor wasn't entirely free. Grace promised to feed her dinner every night she worked.

"It's not really any different than some of the people you put up with at the bar," Grace said before she'd gotten too far away. "Except here, they aren't usually drunk."

"I'd rather deal with drunk college kids than people like that any day of the week," Quinn said, tossing a glance back over her shoulder. She grinned to herself when Grace threw a hand up in an *I don't want to hear it* gesture. Quinn set the books on the floor in front of the shelves she'd be working on. Her back was stiff, and she winced as she tried to stretch her muscles. Getting older was definitely taking a toll on her body. Of course hauling kegs and cases of liquor around every day probably didn't help much either. And like her mother always said, getting older was better than the alternative.

It was almost time to close, and Quinn was just about finished shelving the new arrival books when her cell phone rang. When she saw Callie's name on the display, she almost ignored the call. Instead, she answered it and put the phone to her ear.

"What's up, Cal?"

"Jesus, thank God I got you," Callie said, sounding as though she'd been crying.

Quinn shoved the last book on the shelf and sat on the floor. It wasn't like Callie to cry—*ever*. That was more of a

Meg or Beth trait. Quinn couldn't dispel the sense of dread she felt settling over her. She closed her eyes when her vision blurred and her pulse spiked.

"What's wrong?" Quinn asked, terrified of what her sister's response would be, but at the same time, certain she knew what it was. There was only one thing she could think of that would cause Callie to cry. "Mom?"

"She had a heart attack, Quinn."

The tears stung Quinn's eyes and she banged her head against the shelf behind her, hoping to take her mind off what Callie was telling her. It didn't work. She was vaguely aware of Grace kneeling next to her, a hand on her shoulder. When Quinn looked at Grace, she lost it.

"Is she alive?" Quinn tried not to be swayed by the look of concern on Grace's face. Grace was saying something to her, but Quinn was so focused on Callie she didn't hear a word.

"Yes," Callie answered. She was sniffling, and Quinn heard her wiping the tears away. "I just got off the phone with nine-one-one. The ambulance is almost here. They're taking her to Strong Memorial. Will you meet us there?"

"I'm on my way." Quinn disconnected the call and dropped the phone on the floor beside her leg. Her mother couldn't die, damn it. What would she do without her?

"Quinn, honey, what's happened?" Grace asked, sounding frantic.

"Mom…heart attack," Quinn managed between sobs. Grace sat next to her and gathered her into her arms. Quinn rested her head on Grace's shoulder, not even caring that she was getting Grace's blouse wet from her tears. Grace held her, and Quinn let her. It felt good to have someone comforting her, rocking her, smoothing her hair, and telling her everything would be all right, even though Quinn wasn't sure anything would ever be all right again.

"Come on, sweetie," Grace said. She got to her feet and helped Quinn up too. "I'm driving you to the hospital."

"No, you have to be here."

"Like hell I do," Grace said.

Quinn waited by the door while Grace went around doing her end of day stuff, like locking the safe and turning out the lights. She didn't want Grace to leave work and regret losing the money later, but Quinn had to admit it felt good to have someone taking care of her right now.

CHAPTER EIGHT

You called Meg and Beth, right?" Quinn asked as she took a seat next to Callie in the ER waiting room. Grace sat on the opposite side of Callie, and Quinn breathed a sigh of relief. She didn't think she could handle sitting next to her.

On the ride to the hospital, Grace held her hand, and Quinn had wanted to tell her the awful truth about Lauren. To tell her she should dump Lauren and the two of them should be together. She didn't know where those thoughts and feelings were coming from, and she wasn't sure she liked it. On the other hand, she wasn't entirely sure she *didn't* like it either, which was threatening to cause a minor panic attack. The timing was utterly inappropriate, and Quinn knew it, but then again, if her mother didn't make it…

Quinn had turned her head to look out the passenger window and rested her forehead against the cool glass, trying not to let Grace know she was crying. This was what her mother had wanted for years, for her and Grace to be together. She had it in her mind that they were made for each other, and Quinn had always laughed it off. But what if she'd been right? No, not now, she told herself as she squared her shoulders and sat up straight. Once she knew her mother was going to be all right, then she'd deal with whatever this was.

"You know, it really wasn't the most pressing thing on my mind, Quinn," Callie answered, the annoyance in her voice jerking Quinn back to the present. "The only thoughts I had were getting her to the hospital, and calling you. Besides, I hate talking to either one of them. They're so judgmental because, you know, they live such perfect lives. And of course by that, I mean heterosexual lives."

Quinn raked her fingers through her hair in frustration as she stood. A part of her hoped Callie would have taken care of it, but she knew had the situation been reversed, calling her sisters would have been the last thing on her to-do list too.

"I'm going to step outside and call them." Quinn shook her head when Grace started to get to her feet. "If the doctor comes out with an update, one of you needs to come get me."

Grace nodded and settled back into her seat. Quinn watched as Grace put an arm around Callie and held her, Callie's head against her shoulder. Quinn turned and walked away, trying her best to ignore the jealousy just beginning to churn in her gut.

Once outside, Quinn leaned against the wall and tried to calm her breathing. This was crazy. She didn't know what the hell was going on with her emotions, but she needed to get her act together, and quickly. She pulled out her phone, scrolled through her list of contacts, and pushed to call Beth before she could change her mind. If nothing else, the phone call should take her mind off Grace for a few minutes. It rang five times and she was preparing to leave a voice mail when Beth finally answered, sounding out of breath.

"Hello?" she asked, apparently not checking her caller ID before picking up. Or, Quinn thought, it was more likely Beth didn't have her programmed into her cell phone in the first place.

"Beth, it's Quinn." She waited for some kind of response,

but there was none. "I just thought I should call and let you know Mom's in the hospital. She had a heart attack."

"Jesus, how long ago?"

"Is that your way of asking if I waited a few days to inform you?" Quinn asked, barely managing to hold her temper. This was her sister, and she really didn't want to hate her, but Beth always made it so hard to feel any other way. "It happened a couple of hours ago. Callie was either with her when it happened or arrived shortly after. I haven't gotten any details yet."

"Callie?" Beth asked, managing to ooze contempt. "I thought she was living in Atlanta."

"Yeah, well, she was, and now she's not."

"I'll see what I can do to get a flight in the morning."

"Don't strain yourself," Quinn muttered under her breath.

"What?"

"I said call me when you know what time you'll get in. Callie or I will come pick you up at the airport."

"No, no, don't bother. We can get a cab."

"Whatever." Quinn rolled her eyes as the thought ran through her head that Beth simply didn't want to be seen with a dyke, even if it was her sister. She glanced through the glass doors leading into the emergency room. No sign of a doctor yet, and Grace was still holding Callie in her arms. "Can you please call Meg for me?"

"No need. She's here with me. I've got to go, but we'll see you tomorrow."

Quinn held the phone to her ear for a few moments after Beth ended the call. She shook her head and looked up at the sky as she returned the phone to her pocket. She was glad Meg was there, because she really didn't want to have two conversations like that in one evening. She never had fully understood why her two older sisters seemed to have such a problem with her and Callie being lesbians. Their mother had trouble dealing with it in the beginning, but she came around pretty quickly when Quinn had made it clear she wasn't going to let her shut her out the way Beth and Meg had. She shook her head. There was no point in dwelling on it now. She pushed off the wall and went back inside, determined to get some answers as to her mother's prognosis.

"No word yet?" she asked as she took her seat next to Callie again.

"No," Callie answered with a sigh. "What the hell could be taking so long?"

"You know doctors," Grace said in an obvious ploy to lighten the mood. Quinn smiled her gratitude. "They always want to run this test or that test. It seems as though they're determined to rule out everything it isn't before they come up with a diagnosis for what it is."

Quinn looked up and saw a woman wearing scrubs walking toward them. She tried not to let the woman's grim expression cause any doubt. Her mother had to be okay. As far as Quinn was concerned, it was the only acceptable outcome.

"Callie Burke?" the woman asked, her eyes quickly searching all three of their faces as she spoke.

"I'm Callie."

"How is she?" Quinn asked, getting to her feet to stand beside Callie.

"I'm sorry, who are you?"

"Quinn Burke. Linda is my mother too."

"We're sisters," Callie said unnecessarily.

"Of course, I should have seen the resemblance. I'm Dr. Rosen. Your mother has been taken in for surgery."

"Then why are you out here?" Grace asked.

"Another sister?" Dr. Rosen asked.

"No, but Linda has been like a mother to me for half my

life." Grace stood with her shoulders back, almost as though she were daring the doctor to shut her out.

"I'm not your mother's doctor," she said, her attention back to Callie and Quinn. "The doctor did ask me to come give you an update. She needs bypass surgery, and the doctor felt like it couldn't wait for her to come see you beforehand. She's stable, but she has only one working valve in her heart, and it just couldn't continue doing all the work. At this point, there's no reason to think she won't make a full recovery. The doctor will come and give you another update when she's through with the surgery."

None of them said a word as they all took a seat again. Quinn felt exhausted. She closed her eyes and rested the back of her head on the wall behind her. She smiled when she felt Callie put her head on her shoulder. She hoped the doctor was right, and their mother would make a full recovery. Even though she was forty-two, Quinn wasn't ready to lose her.

❖

Quinn jerked awake when she felt a hand gripping her shoulder and her name being called out. Grace was standing above her when she opened her eyes, and for a moment, Quinn wondered if she was dreaming. But then she felt the hard, plastic, and extremely uncomfortable seat she was in and remembered where she was.

"Mom?" she asked, looking around for a doctor. Her eyes landed on the woman standing next to Grace. It was Lauren. And she was in her scrubs. "What's wrong?"

"I've just finished up with your mother's surgery, and she's on her way to recovery as we speak," Lauren said. She glanced at Grace, and Quinn didn't miss the look of concern she tried to hide. Lauren took a seat next to Quinn and turned her body to face her. "Your mother's heart is weak right now. I was able to repair some of the damage, but there's going to need to be at least one more surgery. I just couldn't risk going any further with it today."

"Is she going to make it?" Quinn felt the tears welling up in her eyes, and she wiped them away brusquely. She hated crying, and there was no way in hell she was going to do it in front of Lauren.

"I have no reason to believe she won't," Lauren answered. "From what Grace has told me about her, she's in relatively good health, all things considered. She's not overweight, and she appears to be in decent shape for a woman her age. Her only problem seems to be that she likes greasy food a little too much."

"That's true." Quinn smiled in spite of the somber mood she was in. She glanced around and noticed for the first time Callie was gone. She looked at Grace. "Where's Cal?"

"She went to the cafeteria to find something to eat. I just texted her while you were talking to Lauren."

"When can I see my mother?"

"It will probably be a while before we get her settled in a room." Lauren got to her feet and went to stand by Grace. "I was just telling Grace you should probably go home and get some rest."

"No, I'm not leaving. Not until I can see her and I know she's all right."

"Grace said you'd feel that way." Lauren turned and put a hand on the small of Grace's back to lead her a few feet away.

Quinn watched as they spoke to each other, quietly enough that Quinn couldn't hear what they were saying. Just then Callie came walking through the doors carrying a tray that held three large cups of coffee. Not hospital coffee either, but Quinn's favorite, Dunkin' Donuts. Obviously Callie hadn't found anything to her liking in the cafeteria.

"Lauren?" Callie said, almost softly enough for Quinn not to hear, but she did.

"You know her?" Quinn asked before taking a drink from the Styrofoam cup Callie handed her.

"Not really," Callie answered.

Quinn looked at her, the feeling of dread washing over her before she could even form a reaction to Callie's words. She almost choked on her coffee. Then she laughed, because she had to be wrong. It would be too much of a coincidence, right?

"Please don't tell me you slept with her."

"Okay, I won't tell you."

"Jesus, Callie," she said as she allowed it to finally hit home.

"What?"

"That's Grace's girlfriend."

To Callie's credit, she looked suitably ashamed. Her face went white, and Quinn was worried for a moment she might throw up all over both of their shoes. Quinn was fighting a queasy feeling in her gut herself. She almost lost the struggle when Grace returned and sat next to her. Thankfully, Lauren was walking away toward the elevators and never looked back.

"What's wrong with you two?" she asked. "You both look sick to your stomachs."

"Don't drink the coffee," Quinn told her, latching onto the first thought to cross her mind. She abruptly stood and pulled Callie to her feet. "We'll be right back. Just need some fresh air."

She pushed Callie toward the sliding glass doors that led to the parking lot and finally remembered to breathe once they were outside. She ran a hand through her hair and started to pace. What a fucked-up mess. Quinn knew she had to tell Grace about Lauren sooner rather than later, because if Grace found out she knew about it and didn't say anything, she'd likely never speak to her again.

"I didn't know," Callie said quietly. "She told me she was single."

"There was no way you could have known," Quinn answered. It didn't make the situation any better though. "She was in the bar Saturday night with another woman after telling Grace she had an emergency at the hospital."

"What? Quinn, we need to tell Grace about her."

"No, you do not say a word about any of this. I'll tell her." Quinn didn't know how she was going to do it, but she had to. She wouldn't allow anyone—especially Lauren—to make a fool out of Grace.

CHAPTER NINE

Grace woke up when she felt someone squeezing her fingers. She opened her eyes and lifted her head to see Linda Burke looking back at her. Grace felt a twinge of panic at how tired and worn out Linda appeared, but quickly reminded herself she'd look horrible too after what she'd just gone through. She reached out and brushed a lock of hair off Linda's forehead and smiled.

"How are you feeling?"

"I've felt better," Linda said, her voice sounding strained.

Grace just looked at her for a moment, thinking how frail this usually strong and vibrant woman was. It was funny— Grace had never thought of Linda as being old before, but it was glaringly apparent now in the unforgiving fluorescent lights of the hospital room. Her skin was wrinkled and her gray hair a mess. She felt bad for Linda, who always made sure she looked her best before leaving the house.

"Mom?" Quinn asked from the chair on the opposite side of the bed where she'd been sleeping as well. She stood and leaned over her mother, taking one small hand between her much larger ones. "I've never been so happy to see you."

"Oh, please, I must look a mess." Linda pulled her hand away and swatted weakly at Quinn's forearm.

"You're beautiful, Mom," Quinn whispered. Grace could see she was fighting back tears. Quinn leaned down and kissed her mother's cheek. "I don't know why you keep making me tell you that."

"It's nice to hear," Linda said with a smile. She looked at Quinn and then to Grace before turning to Quinn again. "What happened?"

"You had a heart attack. Callie found you in your apartment and called the ambulance." Quinn shook her head when Linda tried to lift her head and look around the room. "She's here somewhere. I'll have them page her."

"I want to go home," Linda said before closing her eyes.

"It's going to be a few days before that happens," Quinn said, and Linda's eyes flew open again. "You had surgery this afternoon, and the doctor says you're going to need at least one more, maybe two."

"Why?"

"You needed a triple bypass, Mom. The doctor said your heart was too weak to finish much of it today, so she did what she could, and you'll be going back in probably tomorrow or the next day."

"I hope you didn't call Meg and Beth. I don't want them rushing out here."

"Too late. They'll be here tomorrow."

"Damn it, Quinn—"

"I would be pissed as hell if this happened and they didn't call me, Mom," Quinn said.

Grace could tell Linda was relieved and had only wanted to spare Quinn the discomfort of calling the sisters who condemned her and Callie both simply because they were lesbians. She nodded and closed her eyes again.

"You'd better make them go to a hotel, because I don't

want anyone in my apartment while I'm not there," Linda said before promptly falling back to sleep.

Quinn stood motionless for a moment, just watching her mother sleep. Grace moved to stand by her side and took her hand. She urged Quinn back into the chair she'd been sleeping in earlier and knelt on the ground in front of her. Her heart ached for Quinn when she finally looked at her, and she could see the fear in her eyes.

"I can't lose her, Grace," she said as the tears started to fall.

"You aren't going to lose her, honey," Grace said.

"She isn't out of the woods yet. At her age, one surgery is risky enough, but with at least one more to come…" Quinn's voice trailed off and she took a deep breath as she glanced at the bed. "I'm scared out of my mind right now."

Grace stood and went to get the chair on the other side of the bed so she could drag it over in order to sit next to Quinn. She grabbed her hand again and pulled it into her lap as she sat silently, allowing Quinn to cry for a moment. She would do what she could to keep Quinn strong for her mother, but right now she needed someone to hold her hand and let her get the premature grief out of her system.

Linda was a fighter. Quinn knew that as well as Grace did, and she would remember it soon enough. Grace just hoped Quinn could hold it together when her older sisters arrived the next day, because she knew Quinn hated to show any weakness in front of them.

❖

Quinn finally agreed to go home and get some rest when visiting hours were over and the nurses threatened to have her removed by security. Quinn knew they were just joking. Hell, a couple of them were even flirting with her, but her heart wasn't in it. Her mother was asleep for the night, so Quinn decided her own bed would be infinitely more comfortable, especially with the sisters from hell arriving the next day.

She hated that they could put her on edge so easily. She also hated that no matter how much stress they caused her, there was no way she was going to make them stay in a hotel. If they chose to do it on their own, then she'd be fine with it. But she'd never even suggest it, because they were her sisters, and she knew it was exactly what they would do. Quinn didn't want to be anything like Beth or Meg, and she'd always forced herself to be cordial to them, even though they tried her patience almost constantly. Beth especially.

She hadn't told Callie she was going to let them stay at the house. Callie would've had a conniption fit because she didn't have as thick a skin when it came to their sisters. And Beth and Meg knew it too. Beth did everything she could to push Callie's buttons, and inevitably there would be a shouting match, and more than once, pushing and shoving ensued. Never mind that Beth was fifty-four now. Quinn couldn't imagine what it must be like to hold on to so much contempt and hatred for so many years.

Quinn didn't hate either of her sisters. She'd refused to ever let it get that far. She tolerated them when they came to visit on holidays and managed to avoid them most of the time they were there. This time she knew she wouldn't be so lucky.

Grace had taken her back to the bookstore so Quinn could retrieve her car, and Callie had decided to hang around the hospital "just in case" their mother needed one of them. Quinn had the sneaking suspicion she was really only staying there in order to talk to Lauren, but she couldn't very well have said anything about it in front of Grace.

Quinn took a quick shower and was just crawling into her bed when her phone beeped, indicating a text message. Assuming it was Grace, she grabbed her phone and swiped the screen. She didn't recognize the number but she opened the message anyway. It was from Meg. It was their flight information and a plea for Quinn to pick them up at the airport. Before she could think about too much, she fired off a reply.

No problem. C U 2morrow.

She sighed as she put the phone back on the nightstand and turned onto her side. She'd had the impression the last couple of times she'd seen her that Meg seemed to be coming around. Maybe she'd been right. She smiled at the fantasy of having another sister in her life as she drifted off to sleep.

❖

Grace couldn't sleep. For some reason, she was turned on, and she couldn't figure out why. There was certainly nothing from the hectic day that would warrant this state. She tossed and turned for a good hour before finally settling on her back and staring at the ceiling. Her eyes drifted closed as she slid her hand slowly down her torso and under the waistband of her panties. She tried to imagine it was Lauren touching her, but after a few minutes of frustration, decided it just wasn't happening.

Her mind flashed back to the absurdity of her grandmother's innuendo about her and Quinn. The reaction of her body when Quinn's face popped into her mind shocked Grace enough that she jerked her hand away from where it rested on her inner thigh. What the hell?

It wasn't the fact her body responded to Quinn that bothered her, but the *intensity* of the reaction. The throbbing that commenced between her legs couldn't be ignored. She'd fantasized about Quinn before and hadn't thought anything of it. But this felt…different somehow. She couldn't do this. She got up and went to the bathroom to take a cold shower.

Could her grandparents have been right? More than one woman in her past had accused her of being in love with Quinn, and she'd laughed it off, thinking they were all just crazy. But was it possible? She should be excited about a new relationship with a beautiful doctor, but she wasn't. The problem was, she hadn't realized she wasn't until she'd told Quinn about possibly moving to Rochester. Suddenly, the thought of leaving Quinn scared the hell out of her.

Grace stared at herself in the mirror for a few minutes, wondering about the complexities of life. How was it fair that she could possibly be in love with her best friend and not even be aware of the fact? And if her grandparents were right, Quinn felt the same about her. If they knew each other so well, how could they not know this?

The thought crossed her mind that she'd only told Quinn about the possibility of moving to Syracuse to get some kind of reaction out of her. If she was being honest with herself, and apparently she wasn't very good at it, she didn't love Lauren. She wasn't even sure she enjoyed spending time with her. Quinn had been right about one thing—doctors were definitely not her type. She was sure they weren't all like Holly had been, but she wouldn't know it by Lauren.

Grace ran a hand through her hair and sighed, frustrated with the thoughts occupying her mind. If she'd gone out with Quinn when they'd first met, would they still be together, or would they have grown apart like so many young couples seemed to do? Certainly they wouldn't have become such good friends, and because of that, she refused to dwell on what might have been. She shook her head. More than likely this was just some misguided emotion born of the medical crisis Quinn's family was dealing with.

In the morning, everything would be as it was. As it had always been. Still, she couldn't help but want to offer Quinn a place to stay while her sisters were occupying her house. No small feat that, since the apartment she lived in over the bookstore was one big single room.

She got back into bed, determined to fall asleep if it was the last thing she did. And three hours later, she finally drifted off.

CHAPTER TEN

You two can have my room," Quinn said as she walked into her house, Callie, Meg, and Beth following behind. She tossed her keys onto the kitchen table on her way to the fridge for a beer. She could feel Callie's eyes boring into her, as she still hadn't filled her in on the accommodation situation.

"Wait, where are you going to sleep?" Callie asked.

Quinn had her back to them, but she couldn't stop the smile forming at the indignation in her voice. Callie disliked their older sisters as much as she did, and as far as Callie was concerned, she didn't care if Meg and Beth knew it. In fact, Quinn was positive they already did, and they'd never made any attempts to hide how they felt either.

"I'll take the couch." Quinn tossed a beer to Callie and held a couple of bottles out toward Meg and Beth, knowing they wouldn't take them. It was beneath the two of them to drink beer. She put them back when Beth shook her head and gave her a look of disgust.

"I don't know how you can drink that swill," she said as she hung her purse on the back of one of the chairs at the table. Quinn wasn't surprised when she took it upon herself to start going through her cupboards. Beth was pushy and loud, and she'd always been that way. It was good to know some things never changed. "Don't you have any wine?"

"Sorry," Quinn said, twisting off her cap and throwing it into the garbage can a couple of feet from Meg. She took a long drink and threw an arm around Callie's shoulders. "We're just a couple of barbarians. There's beer and there's whiskey. You want something else, the liquor store's a couple miles away, and oops, sorry, they're closed for the night."

It was after ten, and they'd spent most of the day at the hospital after she'd picked them up from the airport early that afternoon. The day had been pretty much nonstop, and Quinn was looking forward to some time to relax. She hadn't talked to Grace all day, and she was feeling out of sorts because of it. The next day wouldn't be any better because their mother was scheduled for a mid-morning surgery.

"I don't know why we couldn't stay at Mom's," Beth said, more to Meg than Quinn, but she failed to keep her voice quiet enough. Something else that remained a constant with Beth. Her quiet voice was louder than most people's normal speaking volume.

"Believe me, I'd have preferred that arrangement myself, but unfortunately, Mom doesn't want anyone staying in her apartment while she isn't there," Quinn told them. She'd really wanted to argue with her mother about that, but thought better of it. An almost eighty-year-old woman facing two more surgeries shouldn't have to argue with anyone. Quinn set her bottle on the counter and went to stand between Meg and Beth, putting her arms around their shoulders and forcing a smile. "Come with me, ladies, and I'll show you where your room is."

"Get your hands off me," Beth said, ducking away from her and slapping at her hands. "Jesus Christ, Quinn."

"Knock it off, Beth," Meg said. To her credit, she didn't pull away from Quinn. She didn't even cringe when Quinn touched her. Was it really possible Meg was coming around?

"How can you let her touch you?" Beth asked, malice in her voice and her posture. She shivered as though there were bugs crawling up her back.

"Fuck you, Beth," Quinn said easily. She was glad she'd set her beer bottle down, because she had the urge to throw something at her oldest sister. "First of all, you're my sisters, so that's just gross, all right? And second of all, even if you weren't my sister…"

Quinn did the shiver thing then, and she seriously felt like there were a colony of ants running across her skin.

"Beyond disgusting," Callie said, finishing Quinn's sentence. "And you could show a little gratitude. Quinn could have insisted you go to a hotel."

"We should have," Beth muttered.

"Nobody's stopping you," Meg said.

"You're suddenly okay with this?" Beth asked, motioning first to Quinn and then Callie. "They're *lesbians*, Meg. They'll try to convert you. Just like Quinn did with Callie."

"Again, I say fuck you, Beth." Quinn shook her head and wanted to say more. Instead, she decided to hold her tongue when she saw the look of shock on Meg's face at what Beth had implied.

Quinn retreated to where Callie was leaning against the counter by the sink. She crossed her arms over her chest as they watched and waited for the two of them to decide what they were going to do. Quinn couldn't care less what they chose to do. No, that wasn't exactly true. Given the option, she'd prefer to sleep in her own bed.

"Do you even hear the things that come out of your mouth? She's our sister, and there's nothing you can do or say that's going to change that, Beth," Meg said, sounding to Quinn like she was fed up. "She's been gracious enough to let us stay with her. She didn't have to do that."

"I don't know if I want to sleep in her bed," Beth said.

"Jesus," Callie said under her breath. Quinn put a hand on her arm to stop her from confronting Beth. Quinn shook her head and Callie relaxed slightly. "What the fuck, Quinn? You're going to let her be like this?"

"She's always been like this, Cal," Quinn told her. That didn't mean it wasn't hurtful to hear Beth say the things she did, but Quinn had learned over the years to block out most of the things Beth and Meg said. Callie was the baby, and therefore hadn't lived with them as long as Quinn had. "Just let her rant."

"Seriously?" Meg asked.

"We don't know what she's done in that bed."

"Don't worry, Beth. I changed the sheets this morning," Quinn said. "I'm pretty sure no bodily fluids soaked through to the mattress."

Quinn had to turn away from them when Callie burst out laughing and leaned into her. The look on Beth's face was priceless. She looked back over her shoulder when she heard Meg laugh too.

"You should see your face," Meg said to Beth. "I'm staying here tonight. You can go to a hotel if you want. Quinn?"

"Yeah?"

"Where's your room?"

Quinn looked at Callie, who just shrugged. Quinn wasn't sure what was going on with Meg, but if they were forging new ground, she didn't want to screw anything up. She picked up Meg's bags and motioned with her head for Callie to grab Beth's before they headed upstairs.

❖

"Quinn?"

Quinn felt a slight pressure on her shoulder but refused to open her eyes. She'd been having a wonderful dream, and she didn't want to wake up. The dream was about Grace, which was a little worrisome, but it hadn't been the first time she'd had a sex dream about her best friend.

"Quinn."

With a sigh, she rolled onto her back and opened her eyes but instantly shielded them with her hand. She was on the couch, and someone had turned the light on so it was shining right on her face. She cleared her throat and slowly moved her hand to see Meg crouched next to the couch. Quinn sat up quickly and rubbed her eyes.

"What's wrong?" she asked, her voice scratchy from sleep. Meg looked as though she was upset. Quinn felt her heart rate quicken at the thought she might have missed a call from the hospital. She sat up and searched the coffee table for her phone. "Is it Mom?"

"No. No, it's not that," Meg answered with a quick shake of her head. She looked away and leaned back on her feet.

"Meg, what's wrong?"

The silence dragged on for so long, Quinn began to get agitated. She sighed loudly and was about to get comfortable again when Meg finally decided to speak.

"I just wanted to tell you I'm sorry."

"Sorry for what?"

Quinn stared at her, certain the skepticism was obvious in her expression when Meg looked at her. She wasn't quite sure what to say because she didn't know what was happening. She'd never had a conversation with Meg that was any more serious than being told to take out the trash. This apology pretty much shocked Quinn.

"I'm sorry for the way I've treated you over the years, and I'm sorry for the things Beth said earlier."

"You shouldn't have to apologize for someone else's ignorance," Quinn told her. She leaned against the back of the couch and patted the cushion next to her. After a moment, Meg stood and took the seat Quinn offered. "Thank you though."

"I know we've both treated you like shit, and I just wanted you to know I feel bad about it. I'd like for us to be more like sisters than we have been." Quinn watched in silence as Meg chewed her bottom lip and wiped tears from her eyes.

"What's made you change your mind?" Quinn didn't really care. She was just happy Meg was reaching out to her. The reasons really didn't matter at this point.

"John, my husband," Meg said as she met her gaze. Quinn felt a subtle stab of pain in her heart. She'd never met Meg's husband. Hadn't even been invited to the wedding. When Meg and Beth came for the occasional holiday, they always came alone, no husbands and no children.

"Is he gay?" Quinn asked, not quite understanding what she was saying. She smiled when Meg laughed and slapped her on the leg. This felt nice, being able to sit and talk with Meg and not have to worry about being judged.

"No, he has a brother who is though," she said when she stopped laughing. She turned serious, and Quinn could see her eyes filling with tears once more. "I'm so sorry it took someone else being in my life to realize you didn't choose this any more than I chose to be straight. Can you ever forgive me?"

"I can try," Quinn said with a shrug, which caused Meg to laugh again. Quinn took a deep breath. "The important thing is that you've realized it at all. And I want to thank you for taking this step. It really means a lot to me. I'd love for us to be closer."

Quinn stiffened when Meg threw her arms around her

neck and kissed her cheek, but the longer Meg held on to her, the more Quinn relaxed and allowed her arms to go around Meg too.

"If I end up staying in town longer than we first thought, John wants to bring the kids," Meg said when she finally pulled away. "We would go to a hotel, so don't worry about them invading your home."

"I get to meet my nieces and nephews?" Quinn was surprised at the lump forming in her throat. "Aren't they grown and living on their own now? It would be awesome to meet them, Meg."

"Another thing I'm sorry for. Not letting you see them. God, I never even told them they had two aunts they hadn't met." Meg smiled sadly and shook her head. "I did tell them before I came out here though. They really want to meet you and Callie."

Quinn didn't know what to say, but realized she didn't need to say anything. Meg was attempting to mend the rift between them, and Quinn was grateful. Now if only Beth would have an epiphany of her own, maybe they could be a real family for the first time.

CHAPTER ELEVEN

Quinn was up before anyone else the next morning. She felt better than she had since she'd gotten the call from Callie about their mother's heart attack, and she knew a large part of it was because of the talk she and Meg had. The other part was because her mother had called and seemed to be in better spirits.

She had just poured herself a cup of coffee when Callie walked into the kitchen.

"What the hell are you doing up so early?" Callie asked as she shuffled her way to the cupboard for a cup of her own. Quinn poured the coffee into the mug she held out, but didn't answer right away. "You're never up before noon."

"When I'm tending bar, yeah, but since I have at least a month off, and I'm helping Grace at the bookstore, I need to maintain a somewhat normal schedule."

Callie closed her eyes and moaned as she swallowed her first sip of coffee. She looked much more awake when she met Quinn's eyes again.

"I thought I heard talking coming from the living room in the middle of the night. Did Grace come by?"

Quinn hesitated to tell her about Meg's change of heart. She somehow felt it was meant to be just between the two of them, but then realized it affected Callie just as much as it did her, and Meg hadn't asked her to keep it to herself.

"Meg woke me up to talk." Quinn went to the table and took a seat. She watched Callie's shocked expression as she made her way over to join her.

"About what?"

Quinn told her everything, and they were both grinning by the end of it. Callie leaned back in her chair and stared at Quinn for a few moments. She glanced toward the stairs when they heard someone moving around.

"What about Beth?" Callie asked.

"I'd appreciate it if you two would refrain from talking about me," Beth said, breezing into the kitchen and not even sparing a look in their direction on her way to the coffeepot. She looked around for a moment before turning toward Quinn. "You don't have an espresso machine?"

"Barbarians, remember?" Quinn said in response. "There's a Dunkin' Donuts down the street."

"Eeew," Beth said. She spun around and got a cup to fill with coffee. "Please tell me there's a Starbucks nearby."

"I don't really pay attention because I refuse to spend five dollars for a cup of coffee." Quinn rolled her eyes, causing Callie to laugh.

"So," Beth said with a smirk as she sat at the table with them. "Where's Juliet?"

Quinn saw Callie bristle at the question out of the corner of her eye. She placed a hand on Callie's forearm when she was certain Callie was about to stand and give Beth a piece of her mind. Quinn had expected this from Beth though, and she didn't let it bother her the way it had the first few times.

"I honestly don't know, Beth," Quinn said with an indifferent shrug. "Where's Brad? Why didn't he come with you?"

Beth jumped to her feet way faster than Quinn imagined she could at the mention of her first husband's name. Quinn barely had enough time to reach out and grab Beth's wrist right before her hand made contact with Quinn's face.

"You fucking bitch," Beth said between gritted teeth. "You know damn well Brad's been out of my life for more than ten years. How dare you bring up his name?"

"Oh, that's right, you're on husband number three now, right?" Quinn asked innocently while thinking how Beth knew damn well Juliet was out of the picture too.

"I think it's number four," Callie said.

"Fuck you both," Beth said before storming out of the kitchen and then the front door.

Callie laughed when they heard it slam loud enough to shake the windows in the kitchen.

"How many times has she been married?" Callie asked.

"She's on number six in the past fifteen years," Meg said as she walked into the kitchen. "You really love pushing her buttons, don't you?"

"She makes it so easy." Quinn rinsed out her mug and leaned against the counter. "She started it this time by bringing up Juliet again. I finally got up the nerve to throw it back in her face."

"Good. Someone needs to." Meg tried to hide her smile but failed.

"Are we all going to the hospital together?" Callie asked. Quinn smiled when she saw Callie squeeze Meg's shoulder briefly as she walked past her.

"Well, assuming Beth took the rental car in her burst of anger, I'd be willing to bet I'll be going with you guys, if that's all right?" Meg said.

"It's perfect," Quinn answered. "The bus leaves in thirty minutes."

❖

Grace stood when she heard the door to Linda's room open. She smiled at Quinn, who walked in ahead of Callie and Meg. She frowned when she didn't see Beth follow them in. Quinn gave her a smile and a wink before leaning over and kissing her mother on the forehead. Linda's eyes fluttered open and she smiled at her daughter.

"You didn't need to come today," she said, looking past Quinn and smiling at Callie and Meg. Grace watched as she searched the area for her oldest daughter. "Where's Beth? Please tell me you haven't locked her in the basement."

"Hey, there's an idea," Callie said in response.

Grace watched in amazement as Meg backhanded Callie in the gut. They were both laughing. What was going on with the Burke sisters? Grace found herself wondering if she'd entered the Twilight Zone. She fully expected to hear Rod Serling's monologue at any moment.

Quinn shifted her weight, a sure sign she was nervous about something. Grace reached for her hand and was relieved when Quinn entwined their fingers and squeezed gently, her way of letting Quinn know she was there for her no matter what. She knew how much Quinn disliked spending time with her two older sisters, and she could only imagine what last night had been like for her.

"Beth and I had a bit of an argument this morning," Quinn told her. "What else is new, yeah? Don't worry about it. I'm sure she's somewhere drinking an espresso and talking to husband number six about what a disgusting lesbo I am."

"Stop it," Linda said, but her affection for Quinn was apparent in the way she looked at her. Grace found herself wishing she had a mother to look at her with so much love. "What did you say to piss her off?"

"It wasn't like that, Mom," Callie said with a shake of her head. "You know how Beth is. She pushed Quinn, and Quinn finally pushed back."

Linda clicked her tongue and closed her eyes. "I so want you girls to get along. Who's going to look after you all when I'm gone if not each other?"

Quinn released Grace's hand and clasped her mother's as she brushed the hair from Linda's forehead with the other hand.

"You aren't going anywhere, Mama," she said quietly. Grace could tell by the waver in her voice that Quinn was fighting back tears. "You're so stubborn you'll outlive all of us, and you know it."

"You're probably right," Linda said with a chuckle.

"On the bright side, Meg and I had a nice talk last night, and we're making progress on recovering a sisterly relationship," Quinn said.

"Oh?" Linda leaned to the left so she could look at Meg, who was standing next to Grace. Grace smiled at Meg, still wondering what was going on. "That makes me happy."

"I'm just going to step out for a moment," Grace said, feeling as though she were intruding on their private family time. "Get some coffee in the cafeteria or something. Anybody want something?"

"I want bacon and eggs for breakfast," Linda said.

"Yeah, but no," Grace said with a shake of her head. "I think the doctor would never let me back in here."

"I'll come with you," Quinn said. She gave Callie's wrist a squeeze before doing the same to Meg. "Give these three a chance to talk about me without me being in the room."

They walked in silence to the elevator, Grace sensing that Quinn needed time to herself. It was one of the great things about a best friend. You just *knew* when conversation wasn't necessary.

"What time did you get here this morning?" Quinn asked after they were seated with paper cups full of coffee. Grace watched her as she removed her lid and poured in one packet of Splenda.

"Maybe half an hour before you got here," Grace answered with a shrug. Quinn nodded, but didn't say any more. "So, you and Meg? Things are good?"

"Yeah, I think so." Quinn stared into her coffee cup as she spoke. "She woke me up in the middle of the night to tell me she was sorry for how she's treated me all these years."

"Wow," Grace said.

"Right?" Quinn chuckled as she sat back and ran a hand through her hair. "Beth, on the other hand…"

"What happened?

"She asked me where Juliet was."

"What the fuck?" Grace kept her voice down and leaned across the table. "What is her problem?"

"She was the one who ran out of the house when I asked her why Brad didn't come with her." Quinn tried to hide her grin, but it was obviously too much to handle. Grace couldn't help but laugh along with her.

"Good for you," she said, placing her hand over the one Quinn had resting on the table. "I'm glad you finally stood up to her."

"Me too."

Grace's pulse quickened when Quinn's hand turned over and their fingers entwined once again. Their eyes met, and Grace felt her stomach flutter. What the hell was going on with her? She just hoped what she was feeling wasn't obvious by her expression. Quinn would no doubt have a field day with that. The teasing would be endless.

Then again, Grace was almost certain she noticed a subtle hitch in Quinn's breathing as they looked at each other. Was it really possible Quinn was feeling the same things? Quinn swallowed and shook her head before pulling her hand away and getting to her feet.

"I should get back up to her room."

"Have dinner with me tonight?" Grace asked before she could stop herself.

"I think I agreed to have dinner with Meg, Callie, and Beth tonight," she answered. "If Beth hasn't already high-tailed it back to Philly, that is. You're more than welcome to join us."

Grace shook her head. She wanted to talk to Quinn about things and didn't think the newfound relationship with Meg could stand it. She knew Beth would freak out. She smiled and thanked her for the invite, but declined. They could talk some other time. After all these years, a few more days couldn't hurt, right?

"I thought you were having dinner with Lauren tonight," Quinn said as she got to her feet.

"I'm going to break up with her."

"Oh?" Quinn seemed surprised, and really, why wouldn't she be? "I'm sorry."

"No need. I've just come to the realization that she isn't the one."

"You'll find the right one someday, Grace," Quinn said with a smile. "I'm sure of it."

Grace nodded and watched Quinn as she exited the cafeteria. The churning in her gut was troubling, and the jumbled thoughts racing through her mind were confusing. Was telling Quinn about her self-discovery the night before really the right thing to do? It had all seemed so clear, but now in the bright light of day, it seemed silly. Could their friendship handle Grace admitting feelings for Quinn if Quinn didn't feel the same way?

The only thought that was clear in her mind as she stood and walked toward the trash can to deposit her empty coffee cup was a response to Quinn's parting statement.

I think I might have already found the one, and I've just been too stupid to realize it.

CHAPTER TWELVE

"Why aren't you at the store today?" Quinn asked Grace as they walked back into Linda's room. Quinn held the door open for her, and Grace smiled at the chivalry Quinn always seemed to display so effortlessly.

"I put a sign in the window to let people know I would be closed for a few days due to a family emergency," Grace said as she walked past her into the room.

"You shouldn't have done that."

"Why? I'm just as worried about her as you are, Quinn. I want to be here for her," Grace said. "For all of you."

"Thank you." Quinn smiled and kissed her on the cheek. She felt her face grow hot, and she hoped to God she wasn't blushing. If she was, Quinn gave no indication.

They walked to Linda's bedside where Meg and Callie were now sitting having a little chat with their mother. Grace went to stand behind Callie and rested her hands on her shoulders. She smiled at Quinn, who was on the opposite side of the bed, and saw she was looking at where her hands were. She met Grace's eyes for a moment before looking away.

They were talking about anything but the upcoming surgery when the door opened. Grace looked in that direction and saw Lauren entering the room, her eyes scanning the chart she held in her hands. When she looked up and saw all of them there, she abruptly stopped her forward motion.

Grace felt Callie's shoulders stiffen under her hands as Lauren walked backward a few steps.

"I didn't realize you had a full house here, Linda," she said, her eyes darting everywhere but at Grace. Grace wondered what the hell was going on and why everyone seemed to be so tense. "I can come back in a few minutes."

With that, she was gone, and Grace headed for the door after her. She stopped when Quinn reached out and grabbed her arm. She looked at Quinn then at the door.

"I need to tell you something," Quinn said softly as she led her away from the bedside.

"Can't it wait, Quinn?" she asked. She really just wanted to talk to Lauren, to end things and get it over with. Now seemed to be the perfect time for it. She had no desire to go through the charade of going on a date with Lauren before telling her.

Quinn appeared to be torn. Grace could see the worry in her eyes and in the frown lines on her forehead. She had the urge to smooth them out, but somehow resisted. Besides, now was definitely *not* the perfect time for that. Quinn finally nodded before releasing her and going back to her mother. Grace took a step toward her before shaking her head and exiting the room.

She looked both directions before she saw Lauren standing at the nurses' station. She headed that way as Lauren turned and faced her.

"Are you all right?" Grace asked.

"Can we talk about it at dinner tonight? I need to get Mrs. Burke prepped for surgery."

"I can't make dinner tonight."

"Tomorrow, then?" Lauren asked with a smile that looked

forced. In fact, Lauren looked as though she were ready to bolt at any moment.

"No," Grace said with a shake of her head. "I don't think we should see each other anymore."

Grace noticed the slight slump in Lauren's shoulders before she turned back to the nurses' station and opened a chart.

"They told you."

Grace had started to walk away, but the words stopped her just as surely as someone standing in front of her would have. She turned back and went to stand next to Lauren, leaning on the counter and facing her.

"Who are *they*?" Grace asked, working to keep her voice down. The last thing she wanted to do was cause a scene in the middle of the cardiac wing. "And what is it you think *they* told me?"

"I was in the bar Quinn works at Saturday night."

"Wait a minute. Saturday night? The night you canceled dinner because of an emergency at the hospital?" Grace was surprised she was maintaining a level of calmness she'd never experienced before. Yes, she was pissed, but a part of her was relieved too. Lauren obviously wanted out of this relationship as well. "Who were you with?"

"It doesn't matter."

"It does." Callie's reaction when Lauren walked into the room came back to her, and she was finally starting to get it. "Was it Callie?"

"No, I just met her the other day. Wait, so neither one of them said anything at all to you?"

"No, but it doesn't matter now, does it? Because you just told me everything I need to know." Grace left her without another word. She hesitated outside of Linda's room, took a deep breath, and went back in.

❖

Quinn looked up when the door opened, and for a moment, she was relieved to see Grace. But then she noticed the look in her eye and she wanted nothing more than to duck and cover. Callie nudged her with her knee.

"She seems okay," Callie whispered. "Maybe Lauren didn't tell her anything."

"Oh, she knows, trust me. She just won't let on in front of Mom. Just be prepared for a verbal smackdown when we leave here." Quinn never took her eyes off Grace as she spoke.

"Maybe we should just stay here all night then," Callie said before collapsing backward in her chair. She sat up straighter when Grace came and stood in front of them both.

"Do you two have some things you need to tell me?" Grace asked, sounding casual. Quinn knew better though. She was seething inside, and Quinn didn't blame her one bit.

"I didn't know—"

"Not here," Grace said through gritted teeth as she shot Callie a look Quinn hoped was never aimed at her. "You two will meet me in the parking lot when they take your mother in for surgery, understand?"

"Yes," Quinn and Callie answered in unison.

Grace went and kissed their mother on the cheek and told her she'd be back to see her later, when she was out of surgery. Quinn was still staring at the door after Grace was gone and her mother looked her way.

"What did you do?"

"I didn't do anything," Quinn answered a little too forcefully. Her mother clicked her tongue and turned her attention to Callie.

"Then it was you," their mother said with conviction in her tone. "What did you do?"

Callie looked at Quinn, but all she could do was shrug. This was her question to answer, not Quinn's. Quinn was busy fighting the need to run after Grace. To apologize for not telling her about Lauren when she first found out about her infidelities. To wrap Grace in her arms and comfort her.

She shook her head in an attempt to dispel the thoughts.

"I think she and Lauren are having a fight," Callie said as she held her hands up in the air. "I didn't do anything."

"Mrs. Burke?" said a man who entered the room wearing scrubs. "I need to take you down to surgery now."

Quinn, Callie, and Meg all kissed her on the cheek and assured her everything would be fine and that they'd all be there waiting for her when she woke up. When she was gone, they all stood there in silence for a moment.

"Well, I need to get some air," Quinn said. She flung an arm across Callie's shoulders and forced her to walk with her. "Why don't you come with me?"

"I'll call Beth," Meg said. "I can't believe she never showed up here this morning."

"Tell her the dyke contingent of the Burke clan says hello," Callie said over her shoulder as Quinn tightened her grip and led her out of the room before Meg could say anything, but Quinn heard her laugh.

They were quiet on the elevator down to the ground floor. Quinn couldn't help beating herself up about not telling Grace what she knew about Lauren as soon as she knew it. She wouldn't blame Grace if she never wanted to speak to her again. She hoped that wouldn't be the outcome of this mess, but if it was, there wasn't much she could do about it.

They were almost to the door that would take them to the

parking lot when Callie suddenly stopped and pulled Quinn to the side, out of the direct path of foot traffic.

"What's wrong?" Quinn asked. Callie was a strange shade of pale Quinn had never seen before. "Are you all right?"

"Does Grace have any guns?" Callie asked quietly.

"No," Quinn answered, but then she thought about it. "I don't think she does. She's never said anything one way or the other about guns. Wait, are you afraid of her? The big bad homicide detective is afraid of Grace Everett?"

"Fuck you, Quinn. The world is full of people who get shot by someone they never thought could or would do it."

"All right, listen," Quinn said, deciding teasing Callie wasn't the smartest thing to do at that moment. "She was going to break up with Lauren anyway, okay? So I seriously doubt this is going to be anywhere near as bad as either one of us has made it out to be in our minds. Certainly not as bad as you're making it out to be."

"You're probably right," Callie said, her color finally returning to normal. She took a deep breath and Quinn motioned for them to keep walking. "When did she tell you she was going to break up with her?"

"This morning when we were in the cafeteria."

They stopped walking a few feet outside the doors when they saw Grace sitting on a bench waiting for them. Quinn started walking toward her, Callie right by her side. Quinn hesitated, waiting for Grace to invite her to sit, but when she didn't, Quinn took the portion of the bench to her right. Callie sat on her left, but was as far to the end of the bench as she could get.

"So, who wants to start?" Grace asked, not looking at either one of them.

"I'm sorry," Quinn said quietly. She took a deep breath and let it out through her nose. "I should have told you that she was in the bar with another woman on Saturday. She asked me not to. She said you'd broken up."

"And you believed her?" Grace looked at her then, her eyes flashing with anger, and Quinn flinched. She found herself hoping Grace really didn't have a gun with her. "You don't think that's something I would have told you?"

"I didn't believe her. In fact, I called her out on it in front of the woman she was with." Quinn swallowed hard and wiped her sweaty palms on the legs of her jeans. "She swore to me she was going to drop the woman off and then head right home. She said she was going to make it right with you, and she asked me not to tell you before she could have the chance to do it herself."

Grace was silent as she seemed to be contemplating the feasibility of Quinn's explanation.

"How long were you planning to wait for her to tell me first, exactly?"

"You obviously hadn't seen her between Saturday night and brunch on Sunday," Quinn said before she let out an exasperated breath. "And Monday night at bingo didn't seem like the right time because we were all having fun. And Tuesday all hell broke loose when my mother had a heart attack. When exactly would you have expected me to tell you about it?"

Grace studied her for a moment but said nothing. Quinn shifted in her seat and forced herself not to look away while she waited. Unfortunately, Grace wasn't going to give her a break because she turned and looked at Callie then.

"And you," Grace said as she punched Callie in the arm. Quinn could tell it hurt by the wince Callie made, but to her credit, she didn't complain about it. No doubt Callie figured it was the least she deserved, and was preferable to getting shot. "You slept with her."

"She told me she was single," Callie answered. "How was I supposed to know she was your girlfriend?"

Quinn knew her sister had a point, but she also knew Grace, like many people who have been cheated on, probably wasn't thinking rationally. She put a hand on Grace's arm, but Grace shrugged her off and Quinn backed away. She hadn't needed to though, because Grace was still concentrating on Callie. She wasn't even sure Grace was aware Quinn had touched her at all.

"You just should have known," Grace said.

"You should be pissed at her, not me," Callie said. "When someone tells you they're single, do you generally ask them for some kind of proof? She shouldn't have lied, and *that* is what you should be angry about."

"Grace," Quinn said softly before attempting to touch her arm again. Before Quinn could even register what was happening, Grace was on her feet and towering over her.

"Have *you* slept with her too?"

"What? Jesus, Grace, no," Quinn answered, shaking her head. Whether she was shaking it to emphasize her point or to dispel the imagery Grace's words planted in her brain, she wasn't sure. All she knew was Lauren was definitely not her type, and she would never have slept with her, Grace's girlfriend or not. "I swear to you, I never slept with her."

Grace was pacing now, and Callie moved closer to Quinn so she could presumably talk to her without Grace overhearing. She nudged Quinn in the ribs with her elbow and leaned closer, but never took her eyes off Grace.

"That's what she's pissed about, Quinn."

"What the hell are you talking about?"

"She's worried you slept with Lauren. It doesn't really matter that I did, or anyone else for that matter. All she cares about is if *you* had sex with her."

"Fuck off, Callie," Quinn said as she shoved her away. She was getting tired of her trying to convince her she and Grace should be together. She was reading way too much into the situation. But if that were true, why did Quinn's heart speed up? And the fluttering in her belly? That was something new, and she wasn't sure she liked it in conjunction with her best friend.

"I'm telling you, I'm right. I'd bet my life on it." Callie sat back with her arms crossed over her chest, a smug look on her face. Quinn wanted to punch her, but what good would that do?

"Why is she still your mother's doctor?" Grace asked.

"Trust me, I tried to find a different surgeon," Quinn answered. She'd spent all night that first day her mother was in the hospital looking for surgeons in the area. "From what information I could gather on the Internet, she's the best there is in this area. I guess that's probably why Syracuse is luring her away from here."

"God, I wish she were leaving sooner," Grace said quietly.

"You did break up with her, right?" Quinn asked, and Grace simply nodded. "And you were going to before you found any of this out."

"That has absolutely nothing to do with any of this," Grace said, but Quinn was certain she wasn't angry anymore. The fire had gone out of her. "She didn't know that, and I hadn't made up my mind about it until after you saw her at the bar. Jesus, Quinn, how many women has she cheated on me with?"

Quinn stood and opened her arms, and Grace walked right into them without hesitation. She held her for a few moments before letting go and taking a step back.

"She's not worth it, Grace," Quinn told her. "Good riddance, I say. At least you realized you didn't love her before you moved to Syracuse with her."

"I should have listened to you when you said she wasn't my type."

"Remember that in the future." Quinn smiled at the grin Grace couldn't hide. "I know what's best for you."

CHAPTER THIRTEEN

Grace was sitting alone in the waiting room when Beth finally walked in, looking around the room for her siblings, no doubt. Grace wanted to ignore her, but she knew if it was her, she'd want someone to tell her what was going on. She didn't move right away though, but when Beth turned to leave the waiting area, Grace jumped to her feet and quickly walked over to her.

"Excuse me," she said as she reached out and placed a hand on Beth's forearm to stop her from going. Beth jerked away before turning to face her. "You're Beth, right?"

"Yes," she answered, looking and sounding wary of Grace. "How do you know who I am?"

"Forgive me, I should have known you wouldn't remember me," Grace said, feeling foolish. She probably should have lead with an explanation of who she was. "I'm Grace."

Beth simply stared at her as though she were speaking a foreign language. How in the world did Quinn even tolerate this woman? Grace glanced down the hall hoping to see one of the three other siblings, but luck was so not on her side. Why had they all left at the same time? Quinn was going to pay for this.

"Grace Everett?" she said, hoping to nudge her memory,

but Beth's expression never changed. Grace blew out an exasperated breath. "I'm a friend of Quinn's."

That seemed to do the trick. Beth's eyes widened and she took a step back. Grace wanted to laugh, and she honestly had to fight the urge to do so. The look on Beth's face was priceless. It reminded Grace of a small child who had just discovered something awful. She cleared her throat and looked away for a moment.

"Where is Meg, and what the hell are you doing here?" Beth asked.

"Meg went to the cafeteria to find some coffee, Callie stepped outside for some fresh air, and Quinn went to the restroom," Grace told her, choosing to ignore the second part of her question. "They should all be back soon if you'd care to wait for them."

"With you?" Beth shook her head. "I don't think so."

"Whatever." Grace waved a hand in her direction and turned to go back to her seat. "Fucking bitch."

The last two words out of her mouth were spoken under her breath, and after she'd turned away, so she was certain Beth wouldn't have heard it. Apparently, she was wrong, because Beth followed her.

"What did you say to me?"

"By your tone, I think you probably already know," Grace said with a fake smile. "I won't repeat it."

"You little—"

"Think twice before you say what you're about to say," Grace said, effectively cutting her off. "I've had a really bad day, and I am not in the mood to deal with you right now."

"Aw, what happened? Did your girlfriend dump you?" Beth's singsongy tone took Grace right back to high school and the way the popular girls would tease her all the time.

"Back off," Grace told her. She tried to relax her hands,

but they seemed determined to ball up into fists. She felt her face turning red, and she tried to control her breathing to calm her racing heart. "I won't warn you again."

"You and Quinn deserve each other. I don't know why the two of you aren't married. It is legal everywhere now, right?"

Grace felt her jaw drop as Beth turned away and walked toward the elevators. What the hell just happened there? Even Beth, Quinn's homophobic oldest sister, thought they should be together? Grace fell back into the chair and held her head in her hands. This day had been nothing more than a nightmare so far, and she hoped she would wake up soon.

❖

Grace watched Quinn as she returned to the waiting area a few minutes later. Quinn smiled at her and headed in her direction, but Grace shook her head before pointing at Beth, who was sitting alone a few feet away. Quinn looked torn, and Grace really didn't blame her. If she were Quinn, she wouldn't want to deal with Beth alone either. But to Quinn's credit, she went to her sister.

Callie came in a few seconds after Quinn sat across from Beth, and she made a beeline for Grace, shooting glances over her shoulder every couple steps. She sat next to Grace with a relieved sigh and an easy smile.

"Thank God Quinn got back from the bathroom before I got here," she said.

"You should go talk to Beth too, you know."

"Beth and I don't talk," Callie said. "Anytime we're in a room together, we end up yelling at each other. I prefer to stay far away from relationships that are that unhealthy."

"She's your sister."

"Only by blood." Callie winked at her and nudged her

with an elbow. "She's the reason I found out what it means when they said you can't choose your family."

"You're so bad," Grace said, unable to help but laugh. Callie could always lighten the mood, and Grace loved her for it. "Have you ever physically fought with her?"

"Christ no," Callie said as she gazed up at the ceiling. "She doesn't want to catch it."

"Catch what?" Grace asked, thoroughly confused. Callie leaned closer to her and whispered the answer.

"Lesbianism." They both laughed, and neither could stop when Beth and Quinn looked in their direction in unison. When they finally did stop, Callie leaned close again. "I think she truly believes it's a communicable disease."

"Stop." Grace pushed her away. That was just ridiculous. Was anyone that ignorant in this day and age?

"I'm serious," Callie said, making a cross over her heart. "Ask Quinn if you don't believe me."

"Wow," was all Grace could say in response. She saw Meg come in with four cups of coffee in a cardboard carrier. She went over to Beth and Quinn, and Quinn took the carrier from her after Beth wrestled a cup out of it. Without hesitation, she left the two of them and headed for Grace and Callie. "Does she really think she can catch it?"

Quinn looked perplexed as she handed coffee to both of them and sat next to Grace. She looked to Callie and then back to Grace, evidently hoping for something to put the question into context. Grace removed the lid from her cup and blew on the coffee to help cool it off a little.

"Oh, you mean Beth contracting the lesbian virus?" Quinn asked after a moment. Grace looked at her in disbelief. "Yeah, it's true."

"You have told her it doesn't work that way, right?"

"We've tried, but she won't listen," Callie said. "She's one of those people who thinks she knows all there is to know about anything, and there's nothing you can say to sway her opinion."

"This is ridiculous. What about Meg?"

"Meg's finally coming around," Quinn said with a nod. "Like I said, she and I had a nice chat last night."

"Well, that's something, I guess." Grace flinched slightly when Quinn put an arm around her shoulders. What the hell? They touched like this all the time, so why did it feel like there were butterflies invading her stomach? And why had she never felt this way when Lauren touched her? "Maybe she can talk some sense into her."

"Yeah, I wouldn't count on it," Quinn said with a squeeze to her upper arm. "But I guess there's always hope."

"You should come with us to dinner tonight," Callie said, looking at Grace as though it was the best idea ever. Grace rolled her eyes; she couldn't help herself. "Come on, you could be a buffer for us, although why Quinn agreed to go out anywhere with Beth is beyond me."

"I think I'd rather rip off my own—"

"Fingernails," Quinn said.

"Oh, my God," Callie said with a grin.

"What?" Quinn and Grace both asked at the same time.

"She just finished your sentence." Callie shifted in her seat so she was better facing them.

Grace looked at Quinn, who seemed as surprised as Grace felt. Did they do that all the time? She'd never noticed it before. When Quinn met her eyes, Grace gave her a small smile and shook her head.

"How freaking cute is that? Why aren't you guys together?"

"Callie," Quinn said. Grace noticed the look she gave Callie. It was a look of warning to keep her mouth shut. Grace had seen it and heard the tone before.

"What? Jesus, you're a couple already," Callie said in exasperation. "You just aren't sleeping together. Everyone in the world knows it except for the two of you."

Callie walked out of the waiting area without another word, or even waiting for a response. Grace had the feeling Callie and Quinn had this discussion before, and the idea of it simultaneously thrilled and scared her. Plus, she wasn't sure she was happy about the two of them talking about her when she wasn't around.

"Just ignore her," Quinn said as she pulled her arm away from where it still rested on Grace's shoulders. She was looking at the floor and didn't appear as though she would look up anytime soon. "She likes to play matchmaker."

"I know, but with us?" Grace laughed, but it was a nervous laugh. She didn't find this funny at all. "My grandparents kind of asked the same thing the last time I was there."

"What?" Quinn whipped her head up and looked nervous as hell. Grace thought it was cute, but she didn't want to think it. "You're kidding, right?"

"No," Grace answered. It was her turn to avoid looking at Quinn. She clasped her hands together and leaned forward, her elbows resting on her legs just above the knees. "They said they've noticed the way you look at me sometimes. I don't know what the hell they're talking about though."

"Yeah, it's crazy, right?"

Oh, how Grace wanted to say no, it wasn't crazy at all. Maybe all these people were right, and they should explore the possibility. What if they were meant to be together and they just couldn't see it because they'd known each other so long? Yes, they'd fallen into a comfortable routine and they finished each other's sentences sometimes, but didn't that happen to all people who knew each other so well?

"Definitely crazy," she answered instead.

"Yeah," Quinn said, and Grace thought she heard a tinge of disappointment in her voice. Grace refused to look at her because she was afraid she might see desire in the way Quinn looked at her, and even though she thought she wanted that, she just wasn't sure it was right to want it.

Quinn got to her feet and said something about going out for some air. Grace nodded but didn't look up until Quinn was walking away from her. What the hell was wrong with her lately? It seemed like all Grace wanted to do was hold her and comfort her. And kiss her. And feel the weight of Quinn's body on top of hers.

"Where's Quinn?" Callie asked.

Grace sat up straight and hoped what she'd been thinking wasn't written all over her face. She needed to get a grip on these feelings and recognize them for what they were. It was nothing more than a harmless crush on her best friend, and given time, she'd get past it. Just like she always had in the past.

CHAPTER FOURTEEN

Grace agreed to join them for dinner, and Quinn couldn't have been happier. It could only help to have her there, because Beth probably wouldn't want to be too snarky in front of someone who wasn't family. At least Quinn hoped that was the case.

They were being led to their table when Beth leaned closer to Meg to say something in private but, as always, her inside voice was much too loud, and Quinn couldn't help but overhear what was being said.

"I don't understand why we have to have dinner with *them*," she said, and Quinn took a deep breath in an attempt to calm herself. "And why did *she* have to come along too?"

"Afraid of being outnumbered, Beth?" Grace asked, surprising all of them. Callie let out a bark of laughter, and Quinn smiled.

"Excuse me, but I was having a private conversation with my sister," Beth told her as they took their seats at the table. Beth and Meg sat on one side, Callie and Grace on the other, and Quinn sat at the end of the table.

"Then I would suggest working on keeping your voice quieter," Grace said as she opened her menu. "Because I'm pretty sure everyone in a ten-foot radius heard what you said."

"Bitch," Beth said under her breath—sort of. Quinn was

about to say something in response, but Grace put a hand on her forearm and shook her head. Beth glanced over at them, and Quinn saw she was looking at where Grace's hand was. She nudged Meg and jutted her chin toward Quinn and Grace. "See? Why do I have to be seen with people like that? They shouldn't be touching in public."

"Will you please stop?" Meg said as she gripped Beth's wrist.

Quinn smiled and was happy Grace refused to move her hand. Callie caught her eye and motioned with her head toward Meg and Beth. Quinn shrugged. She definitely felt a lesson in social etiquette coming.

"Why is that okay?" Callie asked, pointing at Meg's hand on Beth's wrist before pointing at Grace's hand on Quinn's arm. "But this isn't?"

"Are you that dense? Meg's my sister."

"She's my sister too, Beth," Callie said. "But nobody in this restaurant knows you're sisters. They might think you're *a dyke*."

The last two words were whispered, and Quinn almost laughed at how quickly Beth pulled her arm away from Meg as she glanced around the dining room to see if anyone was watching them. No one was, of course. Beth picked up her menu and began studying it.

"You're an embarrassment," Meg said quietly. Meg had always been the more levelheaded of the two, but Quinn could see she was getting angrier by the second because of Beth's attitude. Quinn decided to let them hash it out and began looking at her own menu even though she already knew what she was getting.

"What did you say?" Beth asked. She set her menu down quickly and turned in her chair to face Meg. "Are you serious with that shit? You're sitting here with three lesbians, two of whom are exhibiting PDA, and *I'm* the embarrassment?"

"Really, Beth?" Grace asked. Quinn slid down a little in her seat. This was going to get interesting. "Public displays of affection? Quinn is my best friend, and I touched her arm to stop her from lashing out at you. After you called me a bitch, by the way. Believe me when I say I won't make that mistake again. And to think, I used to try to defend you when Quinn would talk badly of you. I thought there was no way anyone could be as ignorant as she claimed you were. I was wrong."

Beth was so pissed now that she was turning red. Quinn noticed Meg covering her mouth to hide her smile. Callie reached across the table as though she were going to take Beth's hand, but Beth pulled it away faster than Quinn thought possible.

"Don't you fucking touch me," she said. Quinn was surprised her voice was actually quiet.

"You do know you can't catch it, right?" Grace said with a laugh. "It's not a virus. You don't seem to have a problem with the waiter."

"Why should I?"

"You can't catch being a lesbian from us any more than you can catch being African American from him," Grace said. Beth just stared at her with a blank expression. "Think about it for a while."

"Well done," Callie said with a high-five that Grace didn't hesitate to return. She turned to look at Quinn. "Why didn't we ever make that argument?"

Quinn just shrugged. Quinn had assumed Beth wouldn't be bright enough to get it. From the look on her face, she'd been right.

"We're leaving," Beth said before standing and slinging her purse over her shoulder. She looked at Meg expectantly. But Meg was looking as though she wasn't going to move for quite some time. "Are you coming, or not?"

"No, Beth, I'm staying here. I'm hungry, and I'm tired, and I just want to go back to Quinn's and get a good night's sleep when we're finished here." Meg didn't tear her gaze away from Quinn's eyes. Quinn looked away when she heard Beth give a frustrated sigh and turn to walk quickly out of the restaurant. "Is she gone?"

"Yeah." Quinn nodded. "Maybe you should go after her."

"Quinn, there's something you need to understand about Beth," Meg told her.

"What's that?"

"She's never going to change." Meg seemed to finally relax for the first time since they'd left the hospital. "Ever."

❖

When they were done eating, Callie rode with Meg back to the house, and Quinn gave Grace a lift to the hospital where her car was still sitting in the visitor parking lot. Quinn hadn't been able to stop thinking about their conversation earlier, after Callie said they were already a couple. She was surprised to hear Grace's grandparents had seen the way she looked at Grace, because she wasn't even entertaining these thoughts the last time she'd gone with Grace to visit them.

Quinn knew she sometimes looked at Grace appreciatively. She was a beautiful woman, and anyone who didn't look at her that way at least once in a while had to be crazy. She thought she'd been able to hide her desire for Grace, but it was clear she'd been wrong about that. Now that they'd opened the metaphorical can of worms, Quinn wasn't sure they could avoid the topic any longer. And honestly, she wasn't sure she wanted to.

Except she was. They made the drive back to Grace's car in silence. Quinn wanted to tell her the things she was feeling, but for some reason, she couldn't. How was it possible to feel so nervous around Grace when they'd spent the past twenty years telling each other virtually everything? Quinn *never* felt nervous around a woman, and this feeling was throwing her off-kilter. She pulled into the parking space next to Grace's car and shut off the engine. Neither of them moved to get out of the vehicle, and after a moment, Grace released her seat belt and turned in her seat to face Quinn.

"Maybe we should talk," she said.

"About what?" Quinn asked. She felt stupid asking the question, because what else was there they needed to discuss? She closed her eyes and leaned against the headrest. She wasn't ready to talk about this. "I'm sorry about Beth, but you can't say I didn't try to warn you."

"Quinn." Grace said her name in a near whisper, and Quinn couldn't help but look at her. "That isn't what I meant, and I'm pretty sure you know it."

Quinn's heart hammered in her chest. There was enough illumination from the parking lot lights that she could see Grace clearly. She was smiling at her, and Quinn flinched when Grace's hand touched hers.

"I'm sorry about Callie trying to play matchmaker earlier."

"You need to stop apologizing for other people, Quinn."

"Callie's been trying to get me to admit to feelings for you for years," Quinn said. "My mother too, for that matter. She thinks we should be more than friends."

Grace didn't say anything, but she turned her head and looked out the passenger side window so Quinn couldn't see her face. Quinn didn't know what else to say. What could she say? A part of her hoped Grace would say it wasn't a bad idea, but Quinn knew deep down that Grace no doubt felt the same as she did. *It was wrong.*

"Have you ever thought about it?" Grace's voice was soft, and Quinn wasn't entirely sure she heard her right. Quinn stared at the back of her head, her brain not working properly because she wasn't able to form any words. Finally, Grace turned to look at her.

"Thought about what?" Quinn managed. She closed her eyes and shook her head, wondering where that inane question had come from. "Of course I have, Grace. I asked you out the first time we met, remember?"

"And you haven't given it any more consideration since?"

"You made it clear you only wanted friendship from me," Quinn said, trying to pay attention to the conversation even though her pulse was pounding loudly in her ears. "I think we've done pretty well as friends."

"We have," Grace said with a nod and a smile. "You're my best friend, and you always will be. No matter what. You know that, right?"

Quinn nodded, not fully trusting herself to speak. Grace was the only person in the world who could cause this fluttering in her stomach. She wished to God it wasn't true, but it was. She wanted Grace, and she was sure if they sat there in the car much longer she wouldn't be able to stop herself from kissing her.

"Have *you* thought about it?"

"I'd be lying if I said I hadn't, Quinn," she replied as she reached out and brushed a strand of hair out of Quinn's eye. Quinn couldn't help herself—she leaned into Grace's hand, and Grace responded by cupping her jaw. "I can't tell you how many fledgling relationships ended because I was accused of being in love with you."

Quinn laughed because it was ridiculous, wasn't it? Grace in love with her? She'd never given any indication of it, but then again, Quinn had hidden her feelings pretty well over the years.

"Juliet accused me of the same thing," Quinn said after a moment.

"Is that why she left?" Grace pulled her hand away, and Quinn immediately wanted it back.

"No, she left because she fell in love with someone else," Quinn assured her. "But I guess I can't really say for certain that our friendship had nothing to do with it."

"I should get going," Grace said after a moment. She reached for the handle to open the door, but Quinn stopped her with a hand on her thigh.

"Will I see you here tomorrow?" Quinn asked, tilting her head toward the hospital.

"I don't know, Quinn," she answered, sounding a little uncomfortable. "I'll be here at some point, I'm sure, but I really should open the store up again, don't you think?"

"Of course." Quinn moved her hand away from Grace's thigh as Grace opened the door.

"I'll talk to you soon, okay?" Grace said, leaning back in to look at her for a moment before closing the door.

Quinn simply nodded. She waited until Grace backed out of her parking space before starting her car again. She reached for the gearshift but then let her hand fall into her lap. What the hell had just happened? If Grace had been any other woman, Quinn would have kissed her. But that would have opened a whole new avenue to their relationship, and Quinn wasn't sure either of them were prepared to go down that road. She wasn't sure they ever would be.

CHAPTER FIFTEEN

"How are you feeling?" Quinn asked her mother when they arrived at the hospital the next morning. She took a seat next to her bed, and Callie and Meg dragged other chairs over to sit next to her.

"I've been better," her mother answered with a weak smile. "I feel like I've been run over by a bus."

"The doctor said you're done with surgeries now," Meg said, trying to cheer her up. "If all goes well, she thinks you should be able to go home in a few days. I'm staying here until you're well enough to be on your own at home."

"You don't need to do that," her mother told her.

"That's what I said," Callie added with a shrug. "Who knew she could be so bossy?"

Meg laughed and backhanded Callie in the stomach. Quinn smiled. This was how it was supposed to be with sisters. She hated that they'd wasted so many years, but she hoped they'd have many more to make up for it. Quinn knew Beth was a lost cause, but she was happy Meg had started on the path of healing their relationship. Hell, Beth had even told Meg she wouldn't come to visit their mother until Meg called her every day and told her she, Quinn, and Callie were going out to lunch.

"Where's Grace this morning?" her mother asked. "I haven't seen her, and she's usually here before you are."

"She said she'd be in later to see you," Quinn answered, her pulse quickening at the mention of Grace's name. This had to stop. She felt like a schoolgirl with a major crush on the head cheerleader or something. "She's had the bookstore closed since Tuesday and thought maybe she should open it again before her customers decided she was out of business."

"I've been telling her that for the past two mornings," her mother said. "I'm glad she finally listened to me. And what about Beth? Where is she this morning?"

"Don't know," Meg answered.

"Don't care," Callie added.

"Probably still sleeping," Quinn said. "You know how she likes her beauty sleep."

"What's wrong?" her mother asked. Quinn looked at her sisters, wondering who their mother was talking to. When she looked back at her mother and saw her gaze on her, she sat up a little straighter in her chair.

"Nothing's wrong," Quinn said. She'd often wondered how her mother seemed to be able to read her mind. Not just hers, but all four of her children. It was unnerving. She put on her best grin and shook her head. "Nothing at all."

"Bullshit," their mother said. She looked at Callie and Meg. "Could you give us a few minutes, please? Go find out why they haven't brought me my breakfast yet."

Her sisters left the room, both glancing over their shoulders at her. No doubt Callie was wondering why she hadn't noticed something was wrong with Quinn. When they were gone, her mother pushed a button to raise the head of her bed a little.

"Tell me."

"Nothing's wrong, Mama," she said again.

"You forget how well I know you, honey," she said. "I

can see something's bothering you, so why don't you just tell me?"

Quinn took a deep breath and closed her eyes for a moment. She hadn't been able to stop thinking about Grace since she'd dropped her off at her car the night before. She knew her mother wouldn't let her stay silent for long, so to forestall the speech she knew would come, Quinn began talking. "Callie's trying to push me and Grace together."

"And?"

Quinn stared at her mother for a moment but then shook her head. If she'd been expecting some kind of sympathetic ear, she should have known better. Her mother might be the only person in the world who hadn't tried harder than Callie to get them together.

"We talked about it a little bit last night." Quinn sat back in her chair and ran her fingers through her hair.

"You and Callie, or you and Grace?" her mother asked.

"What good would it do to talk to Callie about it?" Quinn asked, unable to hide her frustration. When she saw the worried look on her mother's face, she regretted her tone. She closed her eyes and took a deep breath before continuing. "Grace and I talked. Bottom line, we both admitted we've thought about it at some point over the years, and she assured me that no matter what, we'd still be friends."

"That sounds like an invitation to me," her mother said.

"Ever since she started seeing Lauren, I can't stop thinking about her." Quinn got to her feet and began to pace at the foot of the bed. She decided to ignore her mother's remark because she was afraid to admit she'd thought the same thing. "She deserves so much better than the women she's chosen to date."

"She deserves you, Quinn, and it's about time you realized it." Her mother held up a hand to stop Quinn from speaking. She waited for Quinn to sit again before continuing. "I know

I've pushed you a lot over the years to be with Grace, but it was because I saw this coming a lot sooner than you did. Grace is a wonderful woman, and it's so obvious that you care very much for each other. The way you two interact reminds me of an old married couple. You both know what the other is thinking, you finish each other's sentences most of the time, and you look at each other with so much love sometimes it's palpable. Honey, you've *never* talked about anyone like you just talked about Grace. Not even Juliet. Think about that for a minute. If you weren't so close to the situation, I know you'd see the same things I do."

Quinn sat there staring at her mother as she talked, realizing the truth of her words even though she wasn't willing to admit it out loud, especially to her mother. She didn't think her mother would tell her *I told you so*, but Quinn didn't want to risk it. Not right now. Right now she just wanted to run away and hide for a few days. She needed to come to grips with the fact she'd allowed herself to fall in love with her best friend. A woman she'd convinced herself would never be any more than that.

Meg and Callie came back into the room then, and Quinn stood to leave. She needed some fresh air. Or maybe to take a long drive. Maybe she just needed the company of an anonymous woman to get her mind off Grace. In fact, the more she thought about it, the better the idea sounded. She'd cut out before dinner and spend some time in a lesbian bar. She was already in the city, so why waste the opportunity?

❖

Grace let out a sigh of relief when it was finally six o'clock and she could lock the doors. She hadn't expected it to be so busy, especially since no one had known she'd be opening the store that day. The steady stream of customers had been good though, because it hadn't given her the time to think about Quinn and the conversation they'd had in the hospital parking lot the night before.

Like she hadn't spent a sleepless night thinking about it anyway. She stretched her tired back and let out a big yawn before beginning her closing routine. She couldn't be certain, but Quinn seemed interested last night. She felt like if she'd tried to kiss her, she wouldn't have resisted. Grace shook her head. That was just crazy. In reality, Quinn probably would have laughed at her if she'd attempted something like that.

Fifteen minutes later, her work was finished and she took the daily deposit to the bank. Once that was done, she sat in her car and tried to unwind from the day. She pulled her phone out and was disappointed to see Quinn hadn't called or texted all day. She decided to shoot a text off to her even though she'd no doubt be seeing her soon at the hospital.

On my way to visit your mom. See you soon?

With every passing second that there was no reply, Grace felt her pulse quicken. Was it possible Quinn was mad at her? Grace didn't think she'd said anything the night before to cause that reaction, but she had kind of left in a hurry after she was the one to suggest they talk. She let out a frustrated sigh and leaned her head back. A full fifteen minutes later, her phone finally vibrated in her hand.

I'm not there. Maybe see you tomorrow.

Grace's heart dropped. Not a question, but a simple statement. Obviously, Quinn didn't want to see or talk to her tonight. They rarely went an entire twenty-four hours without at least talking on the phone. She shook her head and chuckled at herself. Quinn probably just needed some time alone to decompress from dealing with Beth. No big deal, right?

So why did she have an overwhelming feeling of dread?

❖

"Where's Quinn?" Callie asked when Grace walked into Linda's room a few minutes later. "I thought she was going to see you."

"Did she say that?" Grace asked, surprised.

"No, I just assumed."

Grace nodded and forced a smile. "She texted to say maybe she'd see me tomorrow." Grace was careful to not give anything away in her expression, but Callie was looking at her intently.

"What's going on?" Linda asked, interrupting her visit with Meg and Beth to look at her and Callie.

"Nothing," Grace said. "Everything's fine."

"Why do you all insist on thinking I can't tell when something's wrong?" Linda asked, her frustration obvious. "Is it about Quinn?"

"Yes, Mama," Callie answered, ignoring the look Grace gave her. "She left and didn't tell anyone where she was going."

"Is that all?" Linda chuckled and shook her head. "She told me she just needed time alone. Said she was going dancing or something."

Grace sucked in a breath and saw Callie's head turn in her direction from the corner of her eye. God, where was this stab of jealousy coming from? It wasn't something she'd ever experienced before in regard to Quinn. *Going dancing* was Quinn-speak for looking for a one-night stand. It hurt that Quinn felt she needed to do this in order to avoid Grace, but they were just friends, after all.

"You know where she is?" Callie asked quietly when Linda returned her attention to Meg and Beth. Grace nodded her response. Callie stood and grasped Grace's arm to get her to her feet before leading her out into the hallway. "Where is she? Let's go find her."

"No," Grace said. "She obviously wants to be alone. Just let it be, Callie."

"She hasn't been herself all day today. What happened after the two of you left the restaurant last night?"

"Nothing happened. She dropped me off here and we both went home." Grace didn't like lying to Callie. She didn't like lying to anyone, but Quinn and Callie were at the top of her list of people to never tell a fib. She turned to return to Linda's room, but Callie grabbed her arm again, effectively stopping her. "Let it go."

"I can't, okay? I'm worried about her."

"Fine," Grace said, more because she didn't want to argue than anything else. "We'll go to the bar, but we will not let her know we're there, all right? This is only so you can see she's okay."

Callie nodded her agreement before going to tell her mother they were leaving to have dinner. Grace didn't think this was a good idea, and she hoped to God Quinn didn't think she was stalking her. If Quinn saw them, she could blame it on Callie though, since she was the one who insisted they find her.

CHAPTER SIXTEEN

The club was dark when they walked in, and Grace felt Callie's hand on her lower back, more to not lose her in the crowd than anything else, Grace assumed. They made their way to the bar and ordered a couple of drinks. Grace turned and surveyed the dance floor but didn't see Quinn. She was about to give up when she noticed her at a table having what looked like a heated conversation with a woman. Grace could only see the back of the woman's head from where she was standing.

Grace hoped Quinn wouldn't look toward the bar and notice her just as the woman stood and held a hand out to Quinn. Quinn shook her head and Grace watched her lips form the words *no fucking way*. Her gaze shifted to the woman bothering Quinn, and she almost fell over. She felt a steadying hand on her hip and Callie leaned closer.

"Are you all right?" she asked.

Grace shook her head, unable to speak. The woman Quinn was arguing with was Juliet. What the hell was she doing here? Callie followed her line of sight, and Grace knew the moment she saw what Grace was seeing. Callie's hand fell away from her hip, and her body was suddenly tense.

"What the fuck?" she started to walk toward them, but Grace stopped her. "Let go."

"No, I'll take care of it," Grace said, wondering if their usual way of getting rid of unwanted suitors would be welcome tonight. It was obvious Quinn didn't want to dance with Juliet, but Juliet didn't appear as though she was going to give up without a fight. Grace downed the shot of tequila she'd ordered and then a few swallows of beer before heading their way.

Her breath caught when Quinn's eyes met hers and she could tell Quinn was happy to see her. She stepped up beside Juliet, who hadn't even noticed her approach. She took a second to look at Juliet and took notice of the bags under her eyes and the way her hair hung limply across her shoulders. She looked bad, and Grace felt a joy she hadn't expected. She looked back at Quinn and held a hand out to her.

"Sorry I'm late, honey," she said with a huge smile as Juliet focused on her for the first time. If Grace didn't know better, she'd think Juliet was on something. "Let's dance."

Quinn took her hand and stood, pushing Juliet out of the way in the process.

"You," Juliet said in an accusing tone. She looked Grace up and down before looking back at Quinn. "Were you fucking her while we were still together?"

Grace let Quinn's hand go when she felt her start to pull away. She watched as Quinn moved close to Juliet and looked her in the eye.

"What the hell does it matter to you?" she asked. "You were busy fucking someone else and stealing all my money. Get the hell away from me and don't bother me again, or I might be tempted to press charges against you for that."

Juliet backed away from her, and Quinn grabbed Grace's

hand again to lead her out to the dance floor. She was so furious at Juliet she didn't even notice it was a slow song playing. She shook her head and started to back away, but Grace grabbed both her wrists and pulled her closer.

"She's watching," she said in Quinn's ear, causing a sensation of warmth to infuse Quinn's body. Everywhere. "You want this to be believable, right?"

Quinn found herself unable to move when Grace stepped into her, both arms going around her neck. Grace looked into her eyes and Quinn closed hers, willing herself not to think about how good Grace felt with their bodies pressed together. They'd danced like this a thousand times before, so why was it all of a sudden so different? *Because I'm in love with her.* Grace rested her head on Quinn's shoulder and sighed.

Quinn finally placed her hands on Grace's hips as she breathed in the scent of her. It was intoxicating, and no matter how hard she tried to convince herself this was nothing more than a dance, her body was betraying her. Grace's body was swaying with the music, and Quinn felt her nipples tighten.

"I really need a drink," Quinn said before pulling away from her and heading back toward the bar. What the hell was wrong with her? After ordering her drink, she put her elbows on the bar and rested her head in her hands. The thoughts she was having were wrong on so many different levels.

"Hey, sis, are you all right?"

Quinn whipped her head up at the sound of Callie's voice.

"Jesus Christ," Quinn said as she looked over her shoulder and saw Grace walking toward them. All she'd wanted was to spend an evening alone to try to get rid of the feelings she had for Grace. Why couldn't anyone just leave her alone? "What the fuck are you doing here?"

"We were worried about you," Callie said when Grace

stepped up next to her. "And it's a good thing we did come looking for you. Juliet looked like she was trying to sink her hooks into you again."

"Do you really think I'm that stupid?" Quinn asked, standing up straighter and looking back and forth between the two of them. How could anyone possibly think she'd take Juliet back after everything she'd done? "She can try all she wants. Doesn't mean it's ever going to happen."

"Hey," Grace said as she moved closer so Quinn could hear her without yelling. Quinn shuddered at the closeness of their bodies. "We should leave."

"Why?" Quinn was losing the ability to think clearly when Grace put a hand on her shoulder and moved it slowly down her arm until their fingers intertwined. Grace squeezed gently.

"Because you don't really want to be here."

"Yes, I do," Quinn said, trying to pull her hand away, but Grace tightened her hold. She made the mistake of meeting Grace's eyes, and it was all she could do to not close the few inches between them and claim her lips in a kiss. What would Grace think if she knew the thoughts that occupied her mind?

"Give Callie the keys to your car." Grace smiled and shook her head, indicating she knew better than Quinn what she really wanted. "I'll drive you home."

Quinn hesitated. Grace was right, of course. She really didn't want to be there. She'd thought it was what she wanted earlier, but once she'd arrived, all she could think about was finishing her beer and going back home.

Then Juliet had shown up. Tweaked out on something.

Quinn had felt sorry for her, but that didn't mean she'd wanted to talk to her. Or do anything else with her that Juliet suggested. She'd begged Quinn to take her back. Quinn remembered the immense sense of relief she felt when she saw Grace walking toward them.

And then there was the dance. And the way Grace seemed to fit perfectly in her arms. She shook her head to clear the thoughts even as she reached in her pocket and pulled out her keys. She felt as though she weren't in control of anything she was doing. She handed the keys to Callie and allowed Grace to lead her out of the bar.

CHAPTER SEVENTEEN

They were silent on the ride home, and Quinn closed her eyes at some point, obviously asleep. When Grace pulled up in front of the bookstore, Quinn's eyes opened and she looked around like she didn't know where she was.

"I thought you were taking me home," she said.

"I did," Grace answered. She was nervous, and the feeling was foreign to her in Quinn's presence. She didn't like it. They needed to talk things out and see if they were on the same page with everything. Grace couldn't shake the look of desire she'd seen in Quinn's eyes as they talked in her car the night before. "I took you to my home. Not yours."

"Sneaky," Quinn said with a grin that was too sexy for Grace to deal with at the moment, so she looked away. "Now take me to my house. I need to sleep."

"Come upstairs and have a drink with me." Grace opened her door and got out. By the time she reached the door to the bookstore, Quinn still hadn't moved. Grace returned to the car and opened the passenger door for her, waiting patiently for Quinn to get out. Once they were in her apartment, Grace tossed her keys on the table inside the door and went right to the kitchen to pour them both a drink. Scotch sounded good to her right about now.

"I really need to go home," Quinn said when Grace handed her a glass. She set it on the coffee table and stood.

"Quinn, please talk to me," Grace said. She placed a hand on Quinn's cheek and forced her to meet her eyes. "Twenty years is a long time to know someone, yet right now, I feel like we don't know each other at all. We've always talked about everything, right?"

"Yeah," Quinn answered with a nod. She tried to turn her head away, but Grace wouldn't let her. That was when Grace saw something in Quinn's eyes she'd never seen before. Fear. And it scared the hell out of her. "Please, just let me go."

"Not until you tell me what's going on."

Quinn grabbed her wrist and pulled Grace's hand away from her cheek. Grace's pulse quickened when Quinn's eyes focused on her lips, but then Quinn turned and walked toward the door. Grace didn't know what to do.

"Damn it, Quinn," she said, feeling defeated. "Is it something I did? Why won't you talk to me?"

Quinn stopped and hung her head. Grace watched for a moment before going and standing between her and the door. She'd never had many friends worth fighting for, but Quinn was one of them. The only one, really, and she wasn't about to let her walk out while there was something unresolved between them.

"You didn't do anything," Quinn told her, her voice tight with emotion. When Quinn looked at her, Grace was struck by the look of pure need on her face. Quinn took a step toward her, and Grace moved back, but the door stopped her from going far.

Grace knew what was going to happen before Quinn even moved. Everything seemed to go in slow motion. Her back hit the door just as Quinn reached her. Quinn seemed to search her eyes for some sign as to whether or not this was welcome, and

Grace knew she wasn't telling her no. Nevertheless, Quinn took a step back just before their lips touched. Grace had to force herself not to cry out at the loss.

Grace grabbed her by the front of her shirt and pulled her back. Quinn's hands went to the door on either side of Grace's head in order to stay on her feet, and Grace whimpered at the feel of Quinn's lean body pinning her against the door. God help her, she wanted this. And unless she was reading the signals wrong, so did Quinn. How the hell could this be happening? Grace knew she should stop, but stopping was the last thing she wanted.

Her lips found the pulse point on Quinn's neck, and she felt Quinn melt into her. Quinn bent her head slightly so Grace had to pull away, and then Quinn kissed her. It started out gentle, and Grace had the feeling Quinn was giving her an opportunity to break it off. Fat chance. She slid her arms around Quinn's neck and held her tightly against her body as Quinn's tongue brushed along her lips, seeking entry. Grace had the fleeting thought that if she allowed Quinn's tongue into her mouth, everything was going to change dramatically between them.

Then she felt Quinn's tongue sliding slowly along hers, and it suddenly felt like she couldn't get close enough to her. Quinn moved a hand down her side, and when it brushed the swell of Grace's breast, they both moaned.

Damn, Quinn could kiss. Grace had never experienced so much raw emotion and desire in a single kiss before. Then again, maybe she'd never really felt desire before now. Quinn was awakening all sorts of feelings in her body, it seemed. Why hadn't they ever done this before?

Because we're friends, that's why.

The thought was akin to someone throwing cold water on her. Grace broke the kiss and stepped away. She shook her head slowly, wondering if she looked as horrified as Quinn did. Grace wanted to touch her. The need was raw, overwhelming. She'd never been so aroused, and she was embarrassed because it was Quinn who had done it to her. When she reached for Quinn's hand, Quinn moved away.

"Fuck, I'm sorry," she said. "I need to go."

"No," Grace said. She shook her head and didn't move, still blocking the door so Quinn couldn't get out. "No. You don't get to kiss me like that and then run off. We should talk."

"There's nothing to talk about," Quinn said. "I shouldn't have done that."

"In case you didn't notice, I wasn't exactly objecting."

Quinn stared at her. The street below wasn't a particularly busy one, but the sounds seemed amplified in the silence that stretched out between them. Grace leaned back against the door, never breaking eye contact, and Quinn ran a hand through her hair as she shifted her weight from one foot to the other, an obvious sign of her nervousness.

"It's wrong." Quinn's voice was quiet. Kissing Grace had been incredible, but there was no way in hell it could ever happen again. Yes, Grace had kissed her back, but why? Why had either of them allowed this to happen when all that would come of it was a ruined friendship?

"Yeah," Grace replied with a nod, but then she smiled. "But what if it's not?"

Quinn opened her mouth to respond, but nothing came out. It didn't happen often, but Grace was the only woman capable of rendering her speechless. Had Grace wanted this as much as she did? Was it possible? No, no matter how Quinn tried to spin it in her own mind, she couldn't get past the notion it was wrong. You weren't supposed to want your best friend this much, were you?

They always talked about anything and everything. They were always there for each other in good times or bad. They shared a closeness Quinn didn't want to lose, but just as that thought flitted through her mind, she realized something with utter clarity.

That one kiss had changed their relationship, and Quinn feared they'd already lost the closeness they once had. Just because Grace thought she wanted this tonight, it didn't mean she'd still feel the same way come morning.

"You know as well as I do that it's wrong," was all Quinn could think of to say.

"I did at one point. Now I'm not so sure. In fact, right now, I don't think it's wrong at all. It sure as hell doesn't feel like it's wrong."

Quinn knew she must have looked confused, because she sure felt like she was. What was Grace talking about? Just the past few minutes, or had she been struggling with this for a while, as Quinn had been? She didn't pull away when Grace reached for her hand, and she allowed herself to be led to the sofa where they sat side by side. Maybe they did need to talk.

They sat for a few minutes, neither of them speaking, and Quinn took the time to finish the drink Grace had given her. The scotch went down smooth, and she closed her eyes to more fully enjoy it. And, no doubt, to avoid talking about this for just a little bit longer.

"Quinn," Grace finally said, breaking into her enjoyment of the drink she held in her hand. Quinn looked at her and watched as Grace took the glass and set it on the coffee table before moving closer to her and placing a hand on her thigh. "Please talk to me. Tell me what's going on. We didn't talk to each other at all today, and that isn't normal for us."

Quinn considered for a moment how to approach the situation. Should she come right out and tell her she thought she was in love with her, or would a more subtle approach be better? Her mind drifted back to the night before.

"You left pretty suddenly last night," she said after a moment. "Like you didn't want to talk about it anymore."

"I was a little uncomfortable," Grace said. "But only because I wasn't sure what to do with the things I was feeling. I wanted to kiss you."

"Yeah?" Quinn asked, a bit of hope winding its way into her heart. "I wanted to kiss you too. There have been a few times over the years I've wanted to kiss you."

"Why didn't you?"

"You made it pretty clear when we met you only wanted to be friends. I figured if you ever changed your mind about that, you'd let me know." Quinn shrugged and looked away, but when she felt Grace's fingers in the hair at the back of her neck, she turned back to her.

"You've been a wonderful friend to me over the past twenty years, Quinn," Grace said quietly. Quinn's pulse quickened when she saw Grace's eyes move across her face and stop momentarily at her lips before meeting her gaze once again. "But I've changed my mind. I want to be more than friends."

"What if it doesn't work out, Grace? What happens to our friendship then? I don't want to lose what we have. You mean the world to me." There, she'd put her heart on the line and, effectively, put the ball in Grace's court.

"But what if it does?" Grace asked with a grin that made Quinn's heart feel like it stuttered. "Have you thought about that?"

"No," Quinn admitted. She'd never allowed herself the

luxury of thinking about a future with Grace. In her mind, there was no scenario out there that would see them live happily ever after.

"Listen to me." Grace moved so she was sitting on the coffee table facing Quinn, and Quinn had to spread her legs a little to give her the room she needed. She took both of Quinn's hands in her own and their eyes met. "If anything is going to happen between us, we both have to want it, understood? I would hope our friendship is strong enough to withstand a hiccup if things didn't work out. I mean, lesbians stay friends with their ex-lovers all the time, don't they?"

"Um, Juliet?" Quinn asked. No way in hell would the two of them ever be friends.

"And Lauren too, I guess. Huh, point taken. Okay, not *all* lesbians are friends with their exes, but I don't think it would be a problem for us." She smiled and brought Quinn's right hand to her mouth. Quinn's breath caught in her throat when Grace closed her eyes and placed a kiss on her knuckles. "But just let yourself imagine what it might be like if things did work out for us. We'll be wondering why we wasted the past two decades fucking other women when we could have been with each other."

Quinn allowed herself a moment to fantasize, but was quickly brought back to the present when Grace straddled her lap and began a slow movement of her hips. Quinn closed her eyes and tilted her head back as she enjoyed the sensations of this seduction. Each time Grace moved into her, she pulled Quinn's jeans with her, causing them to press against her center. She thought she might explode at any second. She opened her eyes and placed her hands on Grace's hips to still her movements.

"Are you sure this is what you want?" she asked, both

hoping for and dreading an answer in the affirmative. If they ended up in bed, there would be no going back to the way things used to be for them.

"I've never been more sure of anything in my life," Grace answered.

"How do I know you won't regret this in the morning?"

"How do I know you won't?"

"I won't," Quinn said, even though she wasn't really sure of anything except needing to feel Grace's skin against hers. Nothing else mattered now. She moved her hands higher, under Grace's shirt, and moaned at the heat of her skin. A little higher, and Grace raised her arms so Quinn could pull the shirt over her head and throw it on the floor.

Grace arched her back when Quinn leaned forward and kissed her belly. Quinn kissed and licked her way up Grace's torso as her hands moved to her back, quickly releasing the clasp of her bra. She slid it down Grace's arms and their eyes met.

"You're pretty good at that," Grace said with a grin.

"I've had a little practice," Quinn replied before closing her mouth around a nipple. It didn't take long for her to realize that the harder she sucked, the more frantic Grace's grinding in her lap became. She moaned when Grace's hands went to the back of her head and held her against her breast.

"Jesus, Quinn, if you keep this up, I'm going to come." After a few more moments, Grace grabbed her by the hair and pulled her away from her nipple and tried to stop the movements of her hips. She leaned down and rested her forehead against Quinn's. "I don't want to come while we both have far too many clothes still on. Follow me."

Grace stood and held a hand out to her, which Quinn took so Grace could pull her to her feet. Grace started to turn toward the bed, but Quinn tugged on her hand and pulled her back to kiss her. Grace moaned and tried to pull Quinn's shirt out from where it was tucked into her pants.

"You should have told me you could kiss like that," Grace said.

"Yeah?"

"If I'd known, I would have made you kiss me a long time ago."

Quinn stepped back and removed her shirt before they went in for another kiss. Quinn knew she was in trouble when she felt the first sensations of an orgasm building. Grace's tongue was doing incredible things to her mouth, and Quinn wasn't sure she could delay it. She pulled away and shook her head.

"Naked. Now." Quinn made quick work of her remaining clothing, and Grace did the same. Once everything was removed, Quinn stood there staring, unable to make her legs carry her the few feet to the bed.

"Are you okay?" Grace asked, sounding alarmed.

"You are so damn beautiful, Grace. Why did I not know this before?"

"Maybe for the same reason you never told me what a fantastic kisser you are." Grace walked backward toward the bed, and Quinn couldn't help but follow. It was almost as though she had her under some kind of spell. Once Grace was on her back, Quinn crawled onto the bed and then on top of Grace.

Quinn ran her hand slowly down Grace's side to her hip. She was mesmerized by the way Grace reacted to her touch. Eyes closed, head tilted back, and her body arching against Quinn. Quinn began kissing her neck as she moved her hand between their bodies and found the heat between Grace's legs. As her fingers slid through Grace's sex, she moaned and raised up on an elbow, looking down into Grace's face.

"You're so wet," she said.

"It's your fault," Grace responded. "This is what your kisses do to me."

Grace put her hand over Quinn's and moved it down farther, until Quinn was at her opening. Their eyes met, and Grace nodded.

"Please, I need you inside me," Grace said as her eyes slowly closed.

Quinn slid two fingers inside her, and Grace's hands went to Quinn's shoulders. She let Grace set the pace and didn't begin a slow thrust until Grace's hips started moving. Slowly at first, but then her movements became more frantic as Quinn assumed her orgasm started to build. She continued what she was doing with her hand and moved her body down until her face was inches from Grace's center.

She never slowed her thrusts as she ran her tongue around Grace's clit. Grace cried out and Quinn pulled back, worried that something was wrong. She'd never had such a responsive lover before. The air around them seemed to be charged with electricity, and every little touch seemed amplified.

"No," Grace pleaded. She lifted her head to look at Quinn, and Quinn's breath caught at what she saw. Grace's eyes were so filled with need, it was almost primal. Grace let her head drop back to the pillow. "God, Quinn, don't stop. I need you to make me come."

Quinn pulled her fingers out slowly so she could resituate, then used her tongue to explore. Grace was writhing beneath her, and Quinn thought she'd never experienced anything so sexy in her life. Grace wanted this as much as she did. She closed her mouth around Grace's clit and sucked gently. When she was sure Grace was about to go over the edge, she slid her fingers inside again. Grace tightened around them and called out her name as she came.

Quinn crawled back up to stretch out beside her, one hand moving lazily across Grace's abdomen. Grace was breathing heavily, but she wasn't moving. Quinn kissed her shoulder and ran her tongue up her neck to her ear.

"Tell me no one's ever made you come that hard," she said before biting gently on her earlobe.

"No one," Grace said as she finally turned on her side to face Quinn. Quinn ran her fingers through Grace's hair as they looked into each other's eyes. "Or that quickly."

Quinn couldn't help the grin on her face, and Grace laughed before placing a hand on her shoulder and shoving her.

"What was that for?" Quinn asked.

"You look too damned pleased with yourself right now," she answered, and they were both laughing.

"I am."

"You should be." Grace pushed a leg between Quinn's. Quinn sucked in a breath when she felt Grace's thigh press against her center.

Quinn closed her eyes and enjoyed the pressure on her clit as she moved against her thigh. Quinn could tell she was wet and spreading it all over Grace's leg. She didn't care, and Grace obviously didn't either. After a few moments of that while Grace nuzzled her neck and squeezed her nipples gently, Quinn felt her orgasm burst forth in a sensation of intense heat that moved quickly through her entire body. Too quickly.

"Tell me again why we wasted the past twenty years with other women?" Grace whispered in her ear.

"Stupidity?" Quinn asked.

"Stubbornness," Grace countered. She rolled onto her back and encouraged Quinn to snuggle up next to her. Quinn wasn't sure what to do. This was usually the point when she ran out the door. But this time she didn't want to do that. She put her head on Grace's shoulder and an arm across her torso. Grace held her close and kissed the top of her head. "If you'd told me it would be this amazing with you, I'd have jumped into bed with you the day we met."

"Bullshit," Quinn said with a chuckle. She closed her eyes and smiled, knowing sleep would come quickly and easily tonight. "You wouldn't have believed me."

"That's probably true," Grace said. She ran a hand slowly up and down Quinn's back. "I'll see you in the morning."

"Good night," Quinn told her just before she fell asleep.

CHAPTER EIGHTEEN

Grace smiled but didn't open her eyes when she first woke up the next morning. She tried to stretch, but her muscles were sore. The reason why she was sore was what had her smiling. She turned over and opened her eyes, surprised to see Quinn wasn't there. It wasn't even eight o'clock yet, and they hadn't fallen asleep to stay asleep until well after four. A quick glance around the room was all she needed to know Quinn was gone. No need to get up and look for her. The only room that was separate from the rest of the apartment was the bathroom, and the door was wide open, proving to Grace she was alone.

"What the hell?" she said under her breath as she swung her legs over the edge of the bed and got to her feet. She winced at the pain in her muscles, but damn if it wasn't a good kind of pain. She quickly looked for a note, but there was none. It soon became apparent that Quinn had actually run out on her. Like she was nothing more than a one-night stand. "Grow up, Grace."

No, more likely Quinn hadn't felt the need to leave a note because they were such good friends. Grace showered and dressed quickly, deciding she'd run by the hospital before she had to open the store at ten. Because as much as she tried to convince herself that Quinn would be fine this morning, Grace had the niggling feeling in the back of her mind that Quinn wasn't okay with what they'd done the night before.

Grace had expected she'd experience a bit of strangeness about it herself, but she didn't. It felt right to her. It was crazy, but she had the feeling all of her senses were heightened. The biggest thing she noticed were colors seemed brighter and more in focus to her. She chuckled as she got in her car and started the engine.

"You're crazy, Grace," she said to her reflection in the rearview mirror. "Nothing's changed."

But it had. Nothing would ever be the same between her and Quinn again, but as far as Grace was concerned, it was a good thing. She couldn't shake the feeling that they belonged together. That she was finally where she was supposed to be. She just hoped Quinn felt the same way about it.

❖

When Grace walked into Linda Burke's hospital room, it was just past eight thirty. She immediately noticed Quinn wasn't there. Callie and Meg were there, and hell, even Beth was sitting at her mother's bedside. But Quinn was conspicuously absent. Callie looked up when she came in and went to her.

"Where's Quinn?" Grace asked. She allowed Callie to lead her out into the hallway but she was looking for Quinn to come walking toward them. She wasn't.

"I was hoping you knew," Callie said. "She never came home last night. I thought you said you were taking her home."

"I did, but I took her to my place so we could talk." Grace tried not to let the growing panic show on her face. "You haven't seen her at all since we left the bar?"

"No, and I've tried calling her cell phone, and I even tried texting her, but she's not answering." Callie smiled and nudged her with an elbow as they both stood against the wall outside of Linda's room. "So, did she spend the night with you?"

"Yes," Grace answered.

"Finally." Callie blew out a breath and shook her head. "I thought you two crazy kids would never get together."

"Well, obviously we're not together, are we?" Grace felt her agitation rising. "She must regret what happened. When I woke up this morning, she was gone. No note, just gone."

"What time was that?"

"I woke up around seven forty-five. So she left sometime between four and then."

"We left the house about eight, so if she was walking, she probably got there right after we left." Callie pulled her phone out and tried calling Quinn again, and Grace decided to shoot off a quick text to her.

Where r u? I'm at the hospital, figured you'd be here.

"She's still not answering," Callie said as she shoved the phone back into her pocket.

They waited a few minutes to see of she'd reply to Grace's text. When the phone vibrated in her hand, Grace jumped because honestly, she hadn't expected a response.

Had some things to do. Will be by hospital soon.

She showed the text to Callie, who let out a relieved breath. Grace felt a little better after hearing back from her, but she was still a bit worried. "Soon" could mean many things. Quinn knew Grace opened the store at ten, so she might be waiting until after that to show up at the hospital. Or she could be there in ten minutes. Hearing from her obviously made Callie feel better, but the impersonal reply did little to quell Grace's anxiety about Quinn's feelings concerning what they'd done.

❖

"Quinn, what are you doing here?" Taylor asked when she pulled open her front door. "And so early in the morning?"

When Quinn woke up that morning, she'd been uneasy about having had sex with Grace. In the moment, it had felt right, but as was her habit since Juliet left, she'd panicked once the sun came up and she realized she was in bed with someone. No, not just someone this time, she reminded herself. This time it was Grace. And Quinn didn't quite know what to do with the feelings she was experiencing.

"I come bearing gifts," she said with a smile as she held out a cup of coffee and a bag with a couple of doughnuts in it. Taylor took them and motioned her inside.

"Is everything all right?" Taylor asked while she got some napkins and placed a doughnut on one of them for Quinn. She pushed it across the kitchen table so it was right in front of her before taking a seat opposite Quinn. "Thank you for this, by the way."

Quinn watched, amused, as Taylor bit into the Boston cream doughnut. She'd never known anyone who appreciated food as much as Taylor did. It was a wonder she wasn't overweight and out of shape considering all the junk food she consumed.

"You aren't here to tell me you're quitting, are you?" Taylor finished off the pastry and wiped her mouth as she sat back in her chair. "Because I'll have to be honest with you, I'd have to kill you if you are."

"I'm not quitting," Quinn assured her. "I needed to talk with someone about something."

"Well, that's vague," Taylor said as she removed the lid from her coffee cup. "I'm flattered you chose me, but I thought Grace was your go-to person for talking about things."

Quinn ran a hand through her hair and just looked at Taylor, not knowing where to even begin. They'd become friends over the years and had talked about many things, but it had mostly been about Taylor's grief following her wife's death. She was right that Quinn always talked things out with Grace and had never needed another friend to vent with. But this was different. Understanding took over Taylor's features.

"Ah, this is about Grace," Taylor said. Quinn nodded but didn't speak. "You're in love with her, and you don't know how to deal with it."

"Not exactly," Quinn replied uneasily. "We slept together last night, and *that's* what I'm having trouble dealing with."

"Oh, wow, I did not see that coming," Taylor said, but then she chuckled. "Well, actually, I sort of did, but I just assumed it would never actually happen."

"Jesus Christ," Quinn muttered. It wasn't enough that she had to deal with this from Callie and her mother? "You know, I came here because I thought I could get an unbiased view from you, but you sound just like my sister."

"I'm sorry," Taylor said, sounding sincere. She sounded it, but she certainly didn't look it. Taylor took a sip of her coffee and waited for Quinn to continue. But Quinn just sat there with her arms crossed, glaring at her.

She felt bad for snapping at Taylor that way, but she was tired of this crap. It seemed as though everyone she knew was trying to push her and Grace together. After a moment, she relaxed and leaned on the table with her forearms.

"This was never supposed to happen, Fletch," Quinn said, reverting back to the nickname she didn't particularly like. Her late wife was the only one she allowed to call her that. Quinn glanced at her, expecting a reprimand, but Taylor was just watching her with no discernible emotion in her expression. "We agreed we would just be friends."

"I don't understand you sometimes, Quinn." Taylor took another sip of her coffee and sighed loudly.

"Just sometimes?" Quinn grinned because her mother was always telling her the same thing, but never included the *sometimes*.

"Yeah, because usually you make good sense. Did you agree you would be friends, and only friends, forever?"

"It was implied," Quinn said with a shrug. She'd never thought anything other than that, and until the night before, Grace had never given her a reason to think otherwise.

"You're so dense sometimes." Taylor softened her words with a slight smile and shake of her head. "You told me before that when you guys met, Grace was a bit of a player, right?"

"Right," Quinn answered, wondering where this was going.

"When she finally decided she wanted to find someone to settle down with, you were with Juliet."

"Yes," Quinn said, growing impatient, but starting to get it.

"Then, when things went south between the two of you, you decided you were never going to let another woman get that close to you again, because if you did, they'd have the power to hurt you." Taylor looked out the window for a moment before turning her attention back to Quinn. Quinn noticed her eyes filling with tears, but decided not to mention it. "I know the feeling, trust me. I don't think I could stand to lose someone again the way I lost Andrea. But back to your dilemma. So now you're a player. It seems the two of you have never been on the same page as far as what you want out of a relationship."

"We still aren't," Quinn said, but even as she spoke the words, she knew it wasn't true. Eighteen months since Juliet walked out of her life, and she was already tired of the one-night-stand lifestyle. That night Taylor had challenged her to turn down the student in the bar, it hadn't been as difficult as she'd thought it would be.

"You trying to convince me or yourself?" Taylor asked. Quinn looked at her and saw she was trying not to laugh. "Oh, please, if you were still wanting to live like that, there was no way you would have turned down that girl, challenge or not. You forget that I've known you for more than ten years."

"Okay, fine, say we are on the same page," Quinn said. She ran her fingers through her hair and straightened in her seat. "What does that mean?"

"It means people change, Quinn. What Grace wanted from you back then might not be the same thing she wants from you now," Taylor said. "Are you in love with her?"

"I think I always have been, but never let myself think about it too much," Quinn admitted.

"Then I don't understand why you're having such a problem dealing with the fact you slept together."

"It just feels wrong somehow."

"Why? It isn't like you're related or anything." Taylor reached across the table and covered Quinn's hand with her own. "A little unconventional because you've known each other for so long, yes, but I don't think it's wrong. I'm not saying your feelings on it are invalid, but you need to just think about it. Work through why you feel it's wrong."

Quinn didn't need to think about her reason why. It was because they'd been nothing more than friends for so long. They'd grown comfortable in the dynamics of their relationship. Maybe *too* comfortable. Adding sex to the mix just made everything complicated. It changed everything between them.

"I'm worried about losing my best friend if things don't work out," she finally said. She met Taylor's gaze and felt a constriction in her chest she'd never experienced before. Just the thought of losing Grace caused her physical pain. What would happen if her fears came to fruition? She didn't think she'd be able to deal with the fallout.

"Then you need to decide if trying to make a life with her is worth the risk, Quinn. I was devastated when Andrea died. I honestly didn't think I would survive the pain." Taylor wiped her eyes and grabbed a tissue from the box in the center of the table to blow her nose. "But I can tell you now, I wouldn't have given up any of it. I loved her, hell, I still love her. And yet I would do it all over again, I can't even begin to imagine who or where I'd be if it hadn't been for her. Loving her was worth the risk."

Quinn nodded, but didn't trust herself to speak. She'd been there when Taylor had gone through the loss, and she saw how it totally wrecked her. She was just now beginning to return to the woman she'd been when Andrea was alive. Quinn couldn't imagine having to go through that hell herself. Quinn got to her feet and Taylor did the same, coming to her and enveloping her in a hug.

"For what it's worth, I don't think you have to worry about losing your best friend," she said, her mouth close to Quinn's ear. "You two are made for each other."

"Thanks," Quinn said as they stepped away from each other. "When are you going to put yourself back out there?"

"Don't worry about me," Taylor said with a chuckle as they walked to the front door. "I'll get back on the horse when I'm ready. Hey, have you thought about the manager position?"

Quinn looked away, afraid to tell her the piece of paper with the salary amount had gone through the washing machine and the dryer. She'd never even looked at it. She didn't want to admit to Taylor she'd been right in her assumptions.

"I didn't think so," Taylor said with a small smile and a shake of her head. "I hope your mother gets well soon."

Quinn nodded and went out the door, not really feeling a whole lot better about things than she did when she'd arrived. She definitely had some things to think about, and she wasn't entirely sure she could do it while being so close to Grace. In all the time they'd known each other, they'd never gone more than a couple of days without at least talking on the phone, but Quinn needed some distance in order to seriously sort out her thoughts and emotions.

"It feels wrong," she muttered as she walked down the driveway and headed back to her own house. "But is it possible that it's the *right* kind of wrong?" Was there even such a thing? There was a song that said there was, but Quinn wasn't convinced.

CHAPTER NINETEEN

Grace was getting antsy and was beginning to worry that Quinn was doing everything she could to not have to run into her. She was about to leave so she could open the store when Quinn finally walked into Linda's hospital room. She looked at Grace and gave her a small smile before Callie got to her feet.

"Where the hell have you been?"

"Excuse me?" Quinn squared her shoulders, and Grace thought she looked like she was ready for a fight. "Is something wrong with Mom?"

"No, but you didn't come home last night, and you haven't been answering your phone," Callie said. Grace watched as the anger left Callie, and she stood there just looking at Quinn. "I was worried about you."

Quinn took Callie in her arms and gave her a quick hug. She said something in Callie's ear, but Grace couldn't make out what it was. Callie laughed and Quinn smiled as Callie went back to her chair. When Grace managed to catch Quinn's eyes, her smile began to fade. Grace stood and walked over to her, placing a hand on her forearm and leaning close.

"Can we talk for a minute?"

Quinn looked like she was going to say no, but she finally

gave a quick nod and followed Grace out into the hallway. Quinn looked at the floor, at the nurses' station, at a man pushing a gurney down the hallway. Anything to avoid looking at Grace. At least that's what it seemed like to her. Grace took a deep breath and tried to ignore the uneasy feeling in her gut.

"Why do I get the feeling you're trying to avoid me?" she asked.

"I don't know," Quinn answered with a shrug, still refusing to look at her.

"Quinn, I'm not one of your one-night stands," Grace said, her frustration getting harder to keep in check. "You can't just fuck me and then never expect to see me again."

Grace winced at the biting tone of her words, but it was nothing compared to the look of hurt Quinn gave her when she finally met her gaze. God, she wanted to rewind time and take those words back.

"You think I don't know that?" Quinn asked, her voice unsteady.

"Of course I don't," Grace said quietly. "I'm sorry. And I'm sorry that what we did last night made you so uncomfortable you felt the need to disappear before I woke up."

"I'm sorry for doing that," Quinn told her.

"Can we have dinner tonight?"

"Yeah, sure."

They made arrangements to meet and Grace left to go to work. Even though they seemed to leave things in a good light, Grace didn't feel any different than she had earlier. She was worried Quinn was going to shut her out, and she wasn't sure she could handle that. Not now. Not after they'd shared something so intimate. She forced her mind into work mode. Whatever was going to happen was simply going to happen. But she wouldn't give up her friendship with Quinn. Not without a fight. Quinn was too important to her.

❖

"So, tell me everything," Callie said that afternoon when they were finally away from Meg and Beth. Quinn had wanted to get some coffee, and Callie took it upon herself to go with her.

"I don't think I need to," Quinn answered, knowing Grace had no doubt told her she'd spent the night at her place.

"Yeah, I know where you slept last night, but what I don't know is why you ran away this morning."

"I needed to clear my head and think about some things." Quinn paid for both their coffees and found a table to sit at. She grimaced at the bitter taste of the colored water the hospital cafeteria tried to pass off as coffee. "And I needed an objective person to talk to about it all."

Callie looked perplexed, and Quinn almost laughed at her expression. Quinn watched her as she put cream and sugar into her cup and stirred it slowly before leaning back in her seat and making eye contact.

"Who did you talk to?"

"Taylor," Quinn answered. Callie stared at her, blinking rapidly for what seemed liked forever before she spoke again.

"Quinn, what the hell?" she asked, not bothering to keep her voice down. "You went to your boss about this instead of your sister?"

"I think you missed the part where I said I needed an *objective* person to talk to about it." Quinn leaned on the table so she wouldn't have to speak loudly in order to be heard. She also hoped it would let Callie know to be a little more discreet. "You are far from impartial where this particular situation is concerned, am I right?"

"Yes." Callie crossed her arms over her chest and didn't

try to hide the fact she wasn't happy about Quinn going outside the family for advice. "So, what did she say?"

"Nothing I didn't already know," Quinn answered. She chuckled and shook her head. "Probably pretty much the same things you would have said."

"Good," Callie said with a satisfied smirk. "At least you talked to someone who's sensible."

Quinn didn't admit that Taylor had given her a few things to think about. Was Grace worth it? Hell, yes. What she wasn't sure of was whether she was worthy of Grace. And yes, what they'd done last night made her uncomfortable in the bright light of day, but she wasn't exactly sure why. It had been amazing. *Grace* was amazing. But it could never happen again if she had any hope of keeping her as a friend.

"Hey, we're having a cookout tonight," Callie said, pulling her out of her own head.

"Who's *we*? Because last time I checked, it was my house, and my grill, but I didn't know anything about it."

"Meg and I," Callie said. "And Beth actually agreed to come, can you believe it? I think the things Grace said to her at dinner the other night might have gotten through to her. She's been a lot more tolerant."

"I was wondering why she was showing up here when she knew you and I would be here."

"She still doesn't talk to me, but at least she's here." Callie shrugged.

"So there's three of you, and it's a cookout?"

"Why not? Is there a rule somewhere that a cookout has to consist of your entire backyard being filled with people?" Callie laughed. "You should invite Grace. I invited Amanda Rodgers too. Hell, maybe you should invite Taylor. The more the merrier, right?"

"Right," Quinn said, but she was thinking Beth wouldn't

be very happy to be surrounded by lesbians. Actually, the thought gave her a warm, fuzzy feeling. "You invited Amanda? Does that mean they hired you back?"

"Yeah, she called this morning. I told her what's been going on with Mom, and they're going to wait for me to start after she's home and on the road to recovery," Callie said. "So you're stuck with me at least until then."

"You're my baby sister, Cal," Quinn said, even though she was looking forward to having her house to herself again. It probably wouldn't be so bad if Meg wasn't there too, and it seemed Beth would now be around more often as well. "I don't feel like I'm stuck with you. I enjoy having you around."

She hoped if there was a God, He wouldn't strike her down where she sat.

❖

Quinn hadn't called Grace all day. She tried not to let it get to her. They'd made plans for dinner, and Grace had to trust that she'd show up. She figured Quinn wasn't going to be helping her at the store anytime soon because she'd be taking care of her mother, especially after she was released from the hospital, so Grace had called the woman who'd worked for her the previous six years. She'd decided to stop working in order to spend time with her husband, who took an early retirement. Grace was lucky she'd agreed to work part-time for her again through the summer, because she really didn't want to have to train someone new.

She was about to leave at five that afternoon when her phone rang. Expecting it to be Quinn calling to cancel dinner, she was surprised to see Callie's name displayed.

"Hey, Callie," she said, trying to inject a cheery tone to her voice.

"You're coming tonight, right?" Callie asked.

"Coming where?" Grace was confused and didn't even try to hide it.

"Quinn didn't call? We're having a cookout at her place, and you're invited."

"What time?" What the hell, she thought as she locked the front door and headed upstairs to her apartment. Was Quinn really going to stand her up for dinner?

"I'm at the store getting steaks now, so I should be home in about thirty minutes or so, but you can come anytime. Hold on." Grace sat on her couch as she listened to muffled voices. She couldn't make out any words, or even who she was talking to. "Sorry, but you know how it is being a Burke—women try and pick me up wherever I go."

"Jesus, you are so full of yourself," Grace said, but she couldn't help laughing. She and Quinn both could be that way, and Grace probably wouldn't know what to do with either of them if they weren't. "Did you invite her to the cookout too?"

"Damn it, I will as soon as I hang up. You're coming, right?"

Grace thought about it for a moment. Quinn hadn't called to invite her, so what if she didn't want her there? Showing up could cause all kinds of awkwardness. On the other hand, if it was Quinn's intention to stand her up, maybe a little confrontation was warranted.

"I'll be there," she said with a nod. "Just let me grab a shower and get dressed, and I'll be right over."

She wasn't going to let Quinn shut her out. They needed to talk about what happened and where they would go from here, and it needed to be done sooner rather than later. Feeling uncomfortable around her best friend just wasn't acceptable, and she hoped Quinn felt the same way about it.

CHAPTER TWENTY

When Grace walked into Quinn's house forty-five minutes later, she saw Meg and Beth sitting on the couch talking. She wondered for a moment if Callie had told Beth she'd be coming, but then realized she didn't care. Beth's problems were her own, and Grace had enough to worry about without adding someone else's baggage. She waved at them and then headed right for the kitchen and a beer from the fridge. After taking a long drink out of the bottle, she made her way out to the backyard where Callie was tending to the grill.

"Oh, my God, that smells wonderful," she said before giving her a kiss on the cheek. A quick glance around told her they were alone. "Where's Quinn?"

"Probably just getting out of the shower," Callie told her. She tilted her head toward the picnic table. "Could you grab those burgers for me, please?"

Grace picked up the plate and handed it to Callie and she watched as she placed them on the grill and closed the lid. She made a face and shook her head as she sat at the table and motioned for Grace to join her.

"Turkey burgers. You get three guesses who they're for, and the first two don't count."

"Beth?" Grace said.

"You win!" Callie clapped her hands and laughed. She leaned toward Grace and lowered her voice before glancing at the door to make sure no one was coming outside. "The princess refuses to eat red meat."

"Has she always been that way?"

"Nope. Meg said it's just since she met her current husband."

They both looked toward the house when the door slid open, and Grace's breath caught at the sight of Quinn, her hair still wet from her shower, and a tight T-shirt showing off the well-toned muscles in her shoulders and upper arms. She glared at Callie when she heard her chuckle.

"What? I think it's cute she can affect you that way." Callie stood and went back to the grill.

Quinn's step faltered when she saw Grace, and Grace thought she looked like she wanted to turn and run away. At least she had the decency to blush.

"Shit, I forgot to call you," she said.

Grace only nodded, waiting for a plausible excuse before she would even consider talking to her. She watched as Quinn put an arm around Callie's shoulders and said something quietly into her ear. Callie nodded and turned to look at Grace, shaking the spatula at her.

"You two behave, and don't do anything I wouldn't do." She laughed and turned back to the grill.

Grace was surprised when Quinn held a hand out to her. Puzzled, she didn't take it, but looked up into Quinn's face instead. Apparently, her confusion was obvious because Quinn gave her a small smile, the one Grace had always thought was sexier than hell.

"Take a walk with me," she said. Grace nodded and finally slid her hand into Quinn's, the warmth of it comforting her beyond reason.

They walked out to the gazebo Quinn had built herself, which was about fifty feet from the back patio. Plenty of privacy from Quinn's sisters, who were all outside now. They didn't speak on their way there, but Grace noticed how Quinn kept stealing glances at her chest, which was what she was hoping for when she'd intentionally left an extra button undone.

"I'm sorry I forgot to call you about this," Quinn said, looking like she meant it. "I intended to call you when I got home from the hospital, but I got in bed for a quick nap and didn't wake up until Callie got home and made so much noise I thought the entire US Army was in the house. Please forgive me?"

Grace couldn't stay mad at her. In fact, she'd never been able to. She reached out and cupped Quinn's jaw, arousal spiking when Quinn closed her eyes and leaned into her touch ever so slightly.

"You are so beautiful, Quinn," she said as her thumb brushed lightly across her lips. But then Quinn opened her eyes, and Grace saw fear there. She would do anything to take that fear away from her.

"I can't think when you're touching me," Quinn said as she moved away from her.

"And that's a bad thing?"

"Shit," Quinn said, looking down. "Grace, what happened last night—"

"Don't you dare say it shouldn't have happened, Quinn Burke," she said, effectively cutting her off mid-sentence. She thought it might kill her if that was what she was about to say. "I'm not sorry about it and you shouldn't be either. We're both adults, we're both lesbians, and we acted on a mutual attraction. I could never regret what we did."

"So what happens now?"

"What do you want to happen?" Grace held her breath

as she waited for an answer. She wanted to explore this thing between them, wanted to see where it might lead, but she could tell Quinn was spooked about it, and she didn't want to push her into something she didn't want.

"I want things to be back the way they were." Quinn looked up toward the house with a smile and a wave for Meg, who was heading their way.

What the hell did that even mean? Grace forced a smile in Meg's direction, but her mind was reeling. So Quinn did regret what happened between them. She felt a sharp pain in her chest and wondered if that was what it felt like when your heart was breaking. She was vaguely aware of them talking, but she couldn't hear anything they were saying because of the pulse pounding in her ears.

This was ridiculous. They were friends before, and they could get through this. After all, it was just a crush, right? Grace couldn't possibly be in love with Quinn, could she? It was glaringly obvious that Quinn's feelings for her weren't love. Grace wondered what it might be like. Sex after Quinn. Now that Quinn had touched her, she didn't think anyone else could possibly come close to making her feel the way she did. It was certainly true no one before Quinn had made her feel even a fraction of the things she felt last night.

"Grace?" Meg asked as she placed a hand on her shoulder to get her attention. Grace looked up at her, startled.

"I'm sorry, what?" she asked.

"Callie wanted to know how you wanted your steak cooked."

Really? Grace was feeling like her world had just been ripped apart, and Callie was asking about a steak? She shook her head and got to her feet, not even looking in Quinn's direction. She thought if she looked at her, she might lose her resolve.

"I'm sorry, but I just remembered I had other plans tonight," she said, trying to sound sincere. "I need to leave."

She walked quickly back to the house, dreading having to tell Callie she was going. Just before she got there, she decided she didn't need to say anything. She slowed to a normal pace and smiled at her as she walked into the house, Callie no doubt thinking she was getting another beer or going to use the restroom.

Once she was in her car, she had to fight the tears that threatened, and she watched the house, hoping Quinn would come after her and ask her not to go. After ten minutes, it was painstakingly clear that wasn't going to happen, so she started her car and headed back home.

❖

"What about Grace?" Callie asked when Quinn and Meg finally came back up to the patio. "She went inside so fast I didn't get a chance to ask her how she wanted her steak."

Quinn glanced at Meg, who simply shrugged and gave her a sympathetic squeeze on her bicep as she went to sit at the table with Beth again. Callie was looking at Quinn, presumably waiting for an answer.

"She didn't tell you she was leaving?" Quinn finally asked.

"What the hell did you do?"

"Excuse me? Why is this my fault?"

"Maybe because you slept with her last night and now you act as though you don't even want to see her? Could that be why?" Callie set the tongs and spatula down and went into the house.

Quinn didn't want to turn around. She knew Callie hadn't been quiet when she said what she did, and she was sure Meg and Beth were both staring at her. She was not in the mood to deal with them on top of everything else she had on her plate. After a moment, she heard Beth get up and go inside, and then Meg was standing next to her.

"Come sit down," she said as she took her by the elbow and led her to the table. Once they were settled, Meg reached across the table and took Quinn's hand. "Hey, you want to talk about it?"

Quinn felt panic begin to well up inside her. Meg wanted to talk about her love life? Meg, who a week ago was still uncomfortable even being around her and Callie? She guessed it was better than Beth being the one who wanted to talk.

"Why?" she asked quietly.

"Because I'm your big sister, and I missed out on helping you deal with romantic angst when you were a teenager." Meg smiled, and Quinn couldn't help returning it. Quinn fidgeted anxiously, not really knowing what to do with this new sisterly connection she'd never felt before. Meg decided to take pity on her. "So. You slept with Grace?"

Quinn felt her cheeks grow hot, and she knew she was turning red. Meg just grinned and gave her hand a squeeze.

"It's okay," Meg told her with a nod. "I know how sex works. You don't have to be embarrassed, Quinn."

"Yeah, but…" Quinn shook her head and looked down at the table. God, this was awkward. "You and I…we don't…"

"Talk about these things?" Meg asked, and Quinn nodded, grateful she understood. "We've never really talked about anything. You don't have a problem talking to Callie about sex, do you?"

"No, but that's different," Quinn said with a sigh. "She and I…we've always been close."

"Would you rather talk to her now?"

"God, no. Please. She'll tell me what an idiot I am."

"I won't promise not to do the same thing. Was this the first time you and Grace slept together?"

"Yes," Quinn said, knowing she sounded defensive, but not really caring too much. "We're friends. I don't make a habit of sleeping with my friends."

"I'm sorry, but you two have been so close for so long, I just didn't know."

"I didn't want this to happen," Quinn said quietly. It wasn't entirely true, because she'd definitely wanted it to happen. It was just this awkwardness after the fact she hadn't wanted. Somewhere in the back of her mind she knew *she* was responsible for any of the difficulties they might be experiencing now, but she didn't want to think about it. Grace seemed to be okay with everything, but she had to be just as freaked out as Quinn was. At least that was what Quinn was clinging to.

"Okay, then why did it happen?" Meg looked at her, waiting for a response. Quinn had no clue how to answer the question. "Unless one of you forced yourself on the other, then it had to be something you both wanted, at least in the moment, right?"

"I don't think I like getting advice on my love life from my big sister," Quinn told her. "You won't even let me wallow in self-pity."

Meg laughed, and Quinn relaxed a little bit. She even felt herself beginning to smile.

"You need to tell her you're in love with her, Quinn."

"I am not," Quinn lied, not wanting to throw everything out there all at once. Meg shook her head at her. "What?"

"I'm not stupid," she said. "I've noticed the way you look at her."

"I don't look at her any differently than I look at anyone else." Quinn slammed a fist on the table just as Callie came back out to the patio.

"I hope you're happy with yourself," Callie said as she resumed her grilling duties. "I don't know what the hell you said to her, but she's gone."

Quinn had had enough. She was tired of everyone telling her she was in love with Grace and insinuating she looked at her in any special way. This was ridiculous, and she wasn't going to listen to it anymore.

"I've lost my appetite," she said, heading for the door leading back into the dining room.

"Unless you're going to drive to her apartment and apologize for whatever asinine thing you said, then you are staying here and eating dinner with us." Callie never turned around as she spoke.

Quinn sighed and went back to the table. "You think you're my mother now?"

"It's pretty obvious someone has to be," Callie answered. "No wonder you're the only one who's never left the area. You still need Mom to take care of you."

Meg laughed, and Quinn gave her a look that must have conveyed exactly what she'd intended, because Meg covered her mouth and looked away from her. Without another word, Quinn got to her feet and went out to the gazebo so she could be alone with her thoughts. But no more than two minutes later, Meg joined her.

"I'm sorry," she said as she sat down next to Quinn. She coughed into her hand to try to hide the fact she was still laughing. "It was pretty funny though, you have to admit."

"No, I don't have to admit anything of the kind," Quinn said. "Because it wasn't funny. At all. Not even a little bit."

Honestly, Quinn couldn't care less that they were laughing

at her expense. All she could think about was Grace, and how this all seemed so wrong without her there to share in the family being together. She probably did need to apologize to her, but not tonight. Tonight she wanted to get drunk so she didn't have to think about how she was never going to get to feel Grace's skin sliding against hers as they made love again. God, one night hadn't been nearly enough, but then again, it had to be.

"You know, my husband and I were best friends before we started dating," Meg told her.

"Really?" Quinn was surprised, yet also intrigued. "You didn't find it to be weird?"

"Maybe a little, at first, but we never shut each other out. If something was bothering us, we'd talk about it. It was a little awkward in the beginning of our relationship, but we worked through it all together. And a year later, he proposed." Meg smiled the dreamy kind of smile Quinn associated with romance. "You know, it's not a bad thing to be friends with someone before you have sex. Maybe if Beth had tried that, she wouldn't go through men like most people go through Kleenex."

Quinn smiled in spite of herself. She didn't make Meg any promises, but she did agree to think about what she'd said. In that moment, she wasn't sure she was capable of much more.

CHAPTER TWENTY-ONE

Quinn and Callie were sitting on the couch after everyone had either left or gone upstairs to bed. Callie's former, and also future, boss had shown up just long enough to have a drink with them after dinner. Taylor hadn't stayed much longer than that. Quinn didn't want to think about why she'd remembered to call and invite Taylor, but not Grace.

"You haven't called her?" Callie asked after a few moments of sitting in silence.

"No, and she hasn't called me either," Quinn answered, not even thinking about what she was doing as she pulled her phone out of her pocket and checked for messages for what had to be the hundredth time since Grace had left.

"Why should she? She wasn't the one who said something insensitive."

"Fuck you," Quinn said. "Why do you just assume I did?"

"Because I know you, Quinn," Callie answered with a good-natured slap to her shoulder. "And I know I would probably be the one to say something insensitive, so why should I think you'd be any different? Grace always tells us we're more alike than we think we are."

"Well, if I said something insensitive, I don't know what it was."

"And there's the problem. What were you guys talking about out in the gazebo?" Callie asked. "Until Meg went out there, you two seemed to be doing okay."

"About last night, and where we go from here." Quinn sighed and rested her head on the back of the couch. She ran their conversation through her head for the tenth time since Grace left, and she finally got it. "Shit."

"You did say something wrong," Callie said. "What was it?"

"She asked me what I wanted to happen." Quinn leaned forward, her elbows on her knees, and rested her head in her hands. How could she have fucked up so badly? "I told her I wanted things to go back to the way they were."

"Ouch," Callie said with a wince just as Quinn looked at her. "So you basically told her sleeping with her was a mistake. No wonder she took off so fast."

"That wasn't what I meant," Quinn assured her. She wouldn't want to trade what happened between them for anything, but she hated that their easygoing friendship had turned awkward because of it.

"I wasn't even there, and it sounds that way to me. Call her and apologize. It will make you both feel better."

Quinn nodded, but it was almost eleven. Grace was an early riser, and if something woke her up after she'd gone to bed, it was difficult for her to fall back to sleep.

"I can see those wheels turning, Quinn," Callie said with a grin. "Don't worry about what time it is. She needs to know you didn't mean it the way it sounded, and the sooner you do it, the sooner you two might get back to some kind of normalcy."

"I love her, and I don't know what to do about it, Cal," Quinn said, her voice barely above a whisper. She hadn't intended to say the words out loud, but her mouth sometimes worked faster than her brain.

"You tell her, that's what you do about it. The two of you have known each other so long, the transition into a physical relationship should be easy," Callie said. "And it would be if you'd just let it happen."

Quinn pulled her phone out of her pocket and just sat there holding it. She wanted to believe it could be as simple as Callie described it, but she couldn't be sure of anything. She wanted to tell Grace she loved her, but something was holding her back. She just wished she knew what it was.

"I'm heading to bed," Callie told her as she got to her feet. "Call her. I promise you'll feel better once you do."

"Thanks," Quinn said. Callie looked like she was going to say something else, but then turned and went up the stairs. She could easily have rubbed it in that she'd been right all along about Quinn's feelings for Grace. Callie could be annoying that way, but she also knew when to back off. Quinn was grateful it was one of the latter situations this time.

She sat there, not moving, until she heard Callie finish up in the bathroom and her bedroom door closed. Then, before she could change her mind, she dialed Grace's cell. After the fourth ring, the call went to voice mail. She panicked because she had no idea what to say in a message, and shouldn't she make an apology like this in person?

Instead of ending the call, she held on and listened to Grace's voice telling her she couldn't make it to the phone. There was the beep, and Quinn opened her mouth to say something, but nothing came out. She closed her eyes and tried to calm her racing heart.

"Grace, it's me," she said. "I'm sorry for what I said tonight. I didn't mean it the way I think you heard it. Meg was there, and I didn't get to finish what I was saying. Please call me as soon as you can. Good night."

She set the phone on the end table next to her before she

hurried upstairs to brush her teeth. She quickly changed into her sleep shorts and sleeveless shirt and got under the blanket. The problem was, she was wide-awake. Sleep was going to be elusive because she couldn't get the image of Grace, naked, out of her head.

❖

Grace held the phone in her hand until it beeped, indicating there was a new voice mail. She considered not even listening to it. When she'd seen Quinn's name on the display, she almost answered it, but she didn't think she was ready to deal with her right now. She'd come home, heated up a can of soup, and then sat in front of the television all evening. And she couldn't even remember one damn thing she'd watched.

Under normal circumstances, if she found herself in this situation, Quinn would be the one she talked to about it. That wasn't an option now. Quinn was the only close friend she had. There were plenty of people she *knew*, but none she'd even consider talking to about her personal life. Except for Callie. But with Callie, Grace couldn't be one hundred percent sure she wouldn't tell Quinn everything Grace said.

A few minutes after her phone notified her of a voice mail, she sighed and decided to retrieve it. She put it on speaker and listened as Quinn tried to talk her way out of what she'd said. Grace shook her head as the message ended and she deleted it.

"How the hell could it have been anything other than what I assumed it was?" she asked out loud. She put the phone on her nightstand and turned out the light. She knew it was going to take her forever to fall asleep, but she tried to clear her mind and get the images of Quinn out of her head. No easy task, that.

When she opened her eyes again, the sun was out, and the birds were singing. She hurried to get ready for work and spent the time trying not to think of Quinn. She knew she should return her call and give her the opportunity to explain herself, but what was the point, really? Grace knew what she heard, and what she heard was Quinn saying she wished they'd never slept together. She decided not to call her back. At least not yet. Maybe it would do Quinn some good to sit around wondering if Grace was ever going to call back.

By the time she closed the store the next evening, she still hadn't returned Quinn's call. Of course, Quinn hadn't tried her again either. Her stomach was in knots. She almost decided not to drive to the hospital because she wasn't sure she even wanted to see Quinn, much less talk to her. And that was the moment she fully realized things between them would never be the same again. Grace was certain she was falling in love with Quinn, but when had it started?

"Probably the day we met," Grace said under her breath as the elevator doors opened on Linda's floor. She made her way to her room but paused outside the door. Was it even possible that she'd been in love with Quinn for so long? Surely she would have realized those feelings at some point. But then again, she'd gotten fairly adept at convincing herself it was nothing more than a simple crush when those feelings became intense. She took a deep breath and walked into the room, surprised to see Linda was alone.

"Hello," Linda said with a big smile.

"Where is everyone?" Grace asked. She went to the bedside and kissed Linda on the cheek before settling into a chair.

"They were driving me crazy, so I sent them all away." Linda winked and then laughed. "I don't realize what a blessing it is that Meg and Beth live in Philadelphia until all four of them are in a room together. I'm not sure how I managed to raise them."

"They love you; otherwise they wouldn't all be here."

"I know they do, and I love them too, but they certainly know how to make me bonkers."

Grace just smiled and didn't say anything, and she sensed the mood in the room change. When she looked at Linda, she was staring at Grace intently, and Grace couldn't help but feel uncomfortable.

"What's wrong?" Linda asked.

"Nothing," Grace said, hoping she sounded convincing. "I'm just tired is all."

"Bullshit. Quinn was on edge the entire time she was here. Did you two have a fight?"

"Not exactly."

"Then what exactly?"

Grace felt her cheeks grow hot as she shook her head and looked down at her lap. This was Quinn's mother, for God's sake. She couldn't tell her they'd had sex, could she? Even though she'd always been able to talk to Linda about anything, discussing that would just be too weird.

"You two slept together."

Grace's head whipped up and she met Linda's eyes. How the hell was she able to do that? Grace started to shake her head, but then quickly realized lying to Linda would accomplish nothing.

"Yes."

"It's about time," Linda said with a satisfied smirk. "Are you two together now?"

"Hardly," Grace answered with a snort. "Quinn regrets that it even happened."

"I seriously doubt that, dear." Linda was watching her,

and Grace didn't know what to say. Quinn had made it pretty clear the night before. "Whatever's wrong between you, you need to work it out. You're too good together to just throw it all away."

Grace nodded, agreeing with everything Linda said. But what good was it if Quinn didn't agree with it as well? Grace wasn't going to push things with Quinn. Maybe things would eventually go back to the way they were before. The only problem was, she didn't want that, but if that was all she could ever have with Quinn going forward, she'd have to make it be enough.

CHAPTER TWENTY-TWO

After leaving Linda's hospital room, Grace tried for two days to get in touch with Quinn. Every time she'd call, she was sent right to voice mail. It was almost as if Quinn had set her number to not even ring before it went there. She'd gone to the hospital every day, and Linda was due to be released soon, so she knew all the Burke siblings would be rather busy once that happened.

She'd even gone to the house a couple times a day, but Quinn was never there. This was so unlike them, to have gone three entire days without a word to each other. Whether Grace wanted to admit it to herself or not, it was glaringly apparent that Quinn had no desire to see her, or even talk to her for that matter.

It was June, and the vast majority of college students had gone home for the summer. They made up most of her clientele, so this was actually her slow time of year. That was what decided it for her. She was going to stay with her grandparents for a couple of weeks. Maybe that would give Quinn enough time to miss her, and they could get on with being friends again when she got back home. Grace decided she wouldn't call her for the entire two weeks. Why should she when it was so obvious Quinn was avoiding her?

She decided against going to see Linda before she left.

She thought it better if no one knew where she was headed. And if Linda didn't know—or Callie, for that matter—then they couldn't tell Quinn where she was and push her to go after her. If Quinn was going to come after her, it had to be her decision, not anyone else's.

"This is a good thing," she told her reflection in the rearview mirror as she pulled into her grandparents' driveway. Of course, she'd been trying to convince herself of it for the entire drive, and she wasn't any closer to believing it now than she had been two hours earlier. Being away from Quinn felt wrong somehow, and she couldn't shake the feeling. She decided against bringing her things into the house just yet, and she made her way to the front door. As always, the door was unlocked, and she went right on in. She'd have to have another talk with them about the direction the world was heading. It just wasn't safe anymore to leave the doors unlocked all the time.

"Hello," she called out as she walked in, pulling the door closed behind her. There was no answer, so she walked into the living room. No one was home. Maybe she should have called to make sure it was okay to come for an extended visit. She looked out the window overlooking the lake and saw her grandmother on her knees in the garden. She went to the sliding glass door and pulled it open. "Good morning."

"Grace?" her grandmother said as she struggled to her feet and gave her a wide smile. "What on earth are you doing here?"

"I thought I'd just come for a visit, if that's okay." Grace went to her and wrapped her arms around her in a tight hug.

"Of course it's okay," she said. She motioned for Grace to follow her back inside to the kitchen, where she poured them both a glass of iced tea. "It's a very pleasant surprise to have you here."

"Where's Grandpa?"

"Fishing." Her grandmother rolled her eyes. "I swear if he had it his way, he'd be out there every day."

"And you'd be just fine with that, wouldn't you?"

"Probably," she answered, and they both laughed. "It's the only time I have any peace and quiet around here. Of course, I refuse to clean the fish anymore, so whatever he catches, he makes sure they're cleaned and filleted before he walks in the door."

"Good for you."

"I was tired of this place smelling like a fish hatchery all the time."

Grace looked up when she stopped talking, not even realizing she'd been mindlessly stirring her tea with the straw her grandmother had put in it. She gave her a quick smile, but she knew it was too late. The only time Grace played with her straw was when she was seriously upset about something. Without a word, her grandmother took her by the elbow and led her out to the living room where they sat on opposite ends of the couch. Grace took a deep breath and swore to herself she wouldn't cry.

"Why are you here, Grace?"

"I needed to get away," she answered, purposely vague.

"How long are you staying?"

"I don't know. Maybe a couple days. Maybe a couple weeks."

"What happened?"

That's when the tears started, and Grace couldn't stop them. She covered her face with her hands and didn't even notice her grandmother had gotten up until she sat next to her and put her arms around her.

"Honey, please talk to me. What's happened?"

Grace pulled away and reached for a Kleenex from the box

on the coffee table. She blew her nose then shoved the tissue into her pocket. Her grandmother waited patiently, knowing from experience that Grace would only talk when she was ready, and not a second before. Grace found it comforting that someone knew her that well.

Quinn knew her that well.

That started more tears flowing, and Grace got to her feet so she could pace. It was the only thing she'd ever found to stop the crying. She figured it was because her mind was so concentrated on walking, it didn't have the time to think about why she'd been crying in the first place.

"Quinn and I..." She felt the tears start again, so she simply paced faster, back and forth in front of the coffee table. She concentrated on her breathing and shook her head to try to get Quinn's face out of her mind. "We slept together."

Her grandmother said nothing in response, but simply kept watching her pace. Grace stopped and faced her, hands on her hips.

"Aren't you going to say anything?"

"It's about time?" she asked with a small smile. "I don't know what you want me to say, dear."

"Neither do I," Grace admitted right before she resumed her walk. The faster she paced, the angrier she became. How dare Quinn just blow her off like she was nothing more than a one-night stand? Now that she was here, the thought crossed her mind that she shouldn't have left. She should have forced Quinn to face what happened, and to figure out what came next for them.

"Is this something you're happy about?"

"I am. She's not," Grace answered.

"She told you that?"

"She didn't have to." Grace stopped pacing and took her

seat on the couch again, feeling physical and mental exhaustion threatening to take over. "She's been avoiding me."

"So you haven't seen her since it happened?"

Grace hadn't expected so many questions from her grandmother. She'd thought she could just tell her what happened, and she'd take her side. It was sounding suspiciously like she was trying to take Quinn's side in this.

"I have, but I haven't seen her in the past couple of days, and I've tried calling her, but she never answers and she doesn't return my calls."

"Have you tried texting her?"

"What do you know about texting?" Grace stared at her. She was in her eighties and refused to get a cell phone. Grace had tried numerous times to talk them both into getting one, just so they could always be in touch with her no matter where they were. She worried about them.

"Nothing," she answered with a laugh. "But I've heard people mention it, and I think I have a pretty good grasp on what it is."

"Yes, I've tried texting her too," Grace said. "She doesn't respond."

"So why are you here? Why aren't you there, trying to get her to talk to you about it?"

"You have no idea how frustrating it is. I've tried to see and or talk to her so many times over the past couple of days, and she manages to avoid me like I'm trying to infect her with a deadly disease or something."

"That doesn't answer my question," her grandmother said softly. "Why are you here?"

Grace contemplated the question. Why was she really there? She'd never been one to run away from anything in her life. But she wasn't running away this time, damn it. Quinn obviously didn't want to see her, so why not disappear for a few days and let her sweat about it for a while?

"Because I want her to see what it feels like when your best friend disappears without a word. Maybe if I'm not around, she'll be able to really think about things, and we can work things out when I go back."

"And if she decides you should continue as nothing more than friends?" her grandmother asked with a hand on her knee. "Will you truly be okay with that?"

"I'll have to be." Grace shrugged and turned her head to look out the window. "I think it will probably break my heart, but I'll have to be okay with it, if it's what she wants."

"Have you told her you're in love with her?"

Grace whipped her head around to look at her, not even trying to hide her surprise. She thought about lying to her, denying she was in love, but lying had never gone well as a kid, and she was pretty sure her grandmother could sense it when she wasn't telling the truth. It only took her about five seconds to decide it wasn't worth it to lie.

"No."

"You need to tell her." She put her hand up when Grace started to protest. "I know you want her to stew about it for a bit, and I can't say as I blame you, but the next time you talk to her, you need to tell her. Because I'm almost positive she feels the same about you."

Grace just stared at her grandmother as she got up and left the room. How could she possibly know what Quinn was feeling when it had been almost a year since Quinn had come here with her? She shook her head and went to look out at the lake. It was so peaceful here. And quiet. Maybe too quiet. She tamped down the urge to walk out of the house and drive back to Brockport. She wasn't sure she could stand it here for very long with nothing to think about but Quinn.

CHAPTER TWENTY-THREE

There was a time, in high school a lifetime ago, when Quinn had wanted to kill Callie. Quinn had been a senior at the time, and Callie was a freshman. Their mother was gone for the weekend, and by that time in their lives, Beth and Meg were out of the picture. Callie decided she was going to throw a party to try to get into the "in" crowd. Why she ever thought that would happen, or why she even wanted to be associated with the assholes who made up the "in" crowd, Quinn never understood.

Quinn knew she should have stopped the party as soon as she found out about it, but she didn't. Instead, she saw it as an opportunity to invite Vanessa, her girlfriend, for a sleepover. They'd been upstairs in her bedroom, and Callie was busy tending to the seven people who had shown up for her party.

Vanessa was finally going to allow Quinn to do more than kiss her, and Quinn was all hormones. Nothing else in the world mattered to her that night. Not even the fact that Callie had managed to sneak into her room just as Quinn had gotten Vanessa's pants off and had her hand between her legs. But when Callie started snapping pictures and laughing, Quinn ended up chasing her through the house threatening to kill her.

And that was exactly the way Quinn was feeling now.

"Why did you even try to call her?" Quinn asked when Callie informed her Grace wasn't taking her phone calls. "This is between the two of us, and you have nothing to do with it. At all."

"Yeah, well, since you aren't doing anything to resolve the problem, I decided to try and help." Callie was pissed at her, but Quinn couldn't find the energy to care. "Jesus, Quinn, have you even noticed that she hasn't been around anywhere for the past three days? She hasn't come over, she hasn't called, she didn't even show up at the hospital the day Mom was released. That isn't like her."

Of course Quinn had noticed. Did Callie think she was stupid? Quinn understood when Grace stopped trying to call, and even when she stopped showing up at the house in an attempt to talk to her. But when she stopped going to the hospital, Quinn had started to get worried. She'd gone by the bookstore and had been surprised to find Maria, the woman who'd worked for Grace for the past few years, running the place.

Maria told her Grace had asked her to take care of the store for a few days while she was out of town on some personal business. No, she didn't know when Grace would be back, and no, she didn't know where she'd gone, but Maria thought she'd said something about Pittsburgh. Which of course made no sense whatsoever to Quinn. Grace had no family in Pennsylvania that she knew of, so why in the world would she have personal business there?

"Yes, I've noticed."

"Really? Because you don't act like you do."

"Stay out of it, all right, Callie?" Quinn headed up the stairs to her bedroom. Now that their mother was out of the hospital, Meg had moved in over there, and Quinn was happy to be sleeping in her own bed once again.

"Quinn," Callie said, following right on her heels all the way up. When they got to the top, Callie grabbed her arm to stop her from disappearing into her room. "Aren't you worried about her?"

"Of course I am." And that was all it took. The fight went out of her, and she no longer wanted to kill her little sister. "But what can I do about it? She obviously doesn't want to talk to me."

"Because you were ignoring her for two days straight," Callie said, letting out a breath that sounded to Quinn like it was full of frustration. "I swear to God, you're both acting like you're in grade school or something. I feel like I'm your older sister right now instead of the baby of the family."

"Whatever," Quinn said with a roll of her eyes as she pulled away from Callie and walked the few feet to her bedroom. Before closing the door, she threw one last comment over her shoulder. "Stay out of it, Callie. Grace and I will deal with this when we're both ready."

"The hell you will," Callie said loud enough for her to hear through the closed door. Quinn listened until she heard Callie go back downstairs before she turned around and leaned against the door.

She couldn't stop the tears from running down her cheeks any more than she could stop herself from sliding down the door to land on her ass. She pulled her knees in close to her body and rested her head on them as she cried.

Quinn had never felt so lost. It had now been five days since she'd seen or spoken to Grace, and this was unprecedented. She hadn't fully realized how intensely entwined their lives were until now. But if Grace didn't want to see her, then she was going to wait her out. Maria hadn't said she'd left for good, just for a few days.

And that was what Quinn chose to cling to for now. Sooner

or later, she would have to come home, and then they would talk about things. But until then, Quinn would wait. No matter how much her heart ached.

❖

Grace was helping her grandmother make dinner when her phone rang again. Callie. Why was she calling so many times instead of Quinn? Quinn hadn't called even once, and this was the third call today she'd received from Callie. With a sigh, she stepped outside and answered it. If she didn't, Callie would no doubt keep calling her.

"Hi, Callie," she said, trying to sound like she didn't have a care in the world.

"Where the hell are you?" Callie asked. "I've tried calling you all day."

Callie was talking in a hushed voice, and Grace felt anxious about all of the reasons Callie might have been trying to call her. She should have sucked it up and answered the first time.

"What's wrong? Is it Linda? Is she all right?" Grace asked, feeling frantic.

"What? No, Mom's fine. She was discharged yesterday. Meg and Beth are staying with her for a couple of weeks to help her out."

"Oh, thank God," Grace said, but then she felt an altogether new type of panic rising up. "Is it Quinn? Has something happened to Quinn?"

"No, Grace, just sit down and relax for a minute. Everyone's fine, okay?" Callie took a deep breath and let it out on a sigh. "We've been worried about you. You disappeared without a word to anyone about where you were going. I was afraid something bad might have happened to you."

"I needed to get away," Grace said when she finally managed to calm her racing heart. As much as she hadn't wanted to talk to Callie about this, she needed to talk to someone, and Callie was the closest thing she had to a best friend, after Quinn. She closed her eyes and pictured Quinn, and she felt herself begin to smile. "I couldn't deal with her not wanting to talk to me. I felt like I was turning into a stalker, and I really don't want to be *that person*."

"I can understand that." Callie was smiling too. Grace could hear it in her voice. "But you need to come home. I don't know how you're feeling, but Quinn's beyond miserable. She won't talk to anyone, and the littlest things set her off. She's not herself without you, Grace."

Grace refused to cry. She felt the same way. Quinn was her rock, and she felt entirely out of sorts without any contact whatsoever. She almost gave in and agreed to drive to Brockport right then, but the reality of the situation crashed into her mind.

"If she wants me, she has my cell phone number," Grace said. "She hasn't tried to call me even once. I'm hanging up now."

"Grace, wait," Callie said quickly.

"What?" Grace asked when she heard Callie plead with her to wait.

"Are you in Pittsburgh?"

Grace allowed herself a small smile. Maria had done well in telling them what she wanted her to. Her intention was to turn them to the wrong place so no one would show up at her grandparents' house looking for her.

"Yes, I am," she lied. "I take it you went to the bookstore and spoke with Maria?"

"Not me," Callie answered. "Quinn went looking for you."

"Really?" Skepticism tainted Grace's voice. She wasn't sure she believed that. Callie was probably just trying to earn points for Quinn. "Did your mother make her go to the bookstore?"

"No, she's worried about you," Callie said slowly. It sounded to Grace as though she were speaking to a small child and had to speak that way in order for her to understand. Callie sighed, and Grace could imagine her running her hand through her hair in frustration. "Listen, I'm not feeding you a line of crap, okay? She'd kill me if she knew I was telling you this. She's not sleeping. She's not eating much. Meg forces her to eat whenever we go over to Mom's. Grace, she's no good without you. When are you coming home?"

Grace thought about it for a moment. She'd only been there for three days, and since Quinn hadn't bothered trying to call her yet, she wasn't convinced enough time had passed for Quinn to thoroughly consider what she wanted.

"I don't know," she answered. "Probably another week at least."

"Fine." Callie sounded defeated. "I'll try and keep her alive until then. Will you at least call her and let her know you're all right? Maybe then she could at least get some sleep."

"I'll think about it, but she has my number too, you know. Nobody's stopping her from calling me."

"I guess all I can ask is for you to think about it. But please, hurry home. The sooner you get back here, the sooner things can maybe get back to normal."

They said their good-byes and Grace stood on the deck after ending the call. She leaned against the railing and looked out at the lake, so peaceful today. It had turned over recently and still had the murky look, and there was still a faint smell of fish in the air. Soon the water would be blue again, and the fishermen would be out full force, her grandfather included.

When she heard the door to the patio open, she put a smile on her face and turned around to face him.

"How are you doing, dear?" he asked.

Grace knew her grandmother had told him what was going on, but she'd also implored him to not bother her while she was staying with them. Grace loved her grandmother, but there was no way he could ever bother her. He was the sweetest, kindest man she'd ever known, besides her brother.

"I'm okay, Grandpa," she replied with a quick hug.

"Are you sure?"

"I am."

"Was that Quinn you were talking to?"

"No, it was Callie," she answered. They'd met Callie a few times before they'd moved here from Brockport. Both of her grandparents seemed to be in love with the Burke sisters, and Grace had always thought it was cute. Of course, they'd pushed on occasion for her and Quinn to be together, but she'd been too close to the situation to see things clearly. She could admit now that she'd been slowly falling in love with Quinn over the years. Not just a harmless crush. And definitely not going away.

"Oh." He looked over her shoulder at the lake. "Maybe you should call her then."

"Maybe I should." But she knew she wouldn't. It was up to Quinn now, and there wasn't anything Grace could do about it.

"Hey, I have an idea," he said with a gleam in his eye. He motioned for Grace to move closer so he could whisper. It didn't seem to matter that her grandmother was inside and couldn't hear what they were saying anyway. "Your grandmother wants to take you to a flower show or some such nonsense tomorrow. What do you say about going fishing with me instead?"

Grace laughed and put her arms around him again. She

loved that he knew she hated flower shows. Or any kind of "girly" type things, for that matter. Her grandmother knew as well, but she seemed determined to have someone share her interests.

"I would love to go fishing with you," she said as she linked her arm through his and they headed back to the house. "But you're telling her."

"You aren't afraid of her, are you?" he asked with a laugh.

"No more than you are," Grace answered, grinning.

"Oh, we're in trouble, aren't we?"

CHAPTER TWENTY-FOUR

Grace breathed in the fresh air and smiled. Since Lake Erie had recently turned over and still wasn't clear, the majority of fishermen were out on Lake Ontario instead. She'd always preferred Lake Ontario anyway, but she'd never tell her grandfather that. He loved Lake Erie, which was why they'd chosen to purchase a house there.

They'd been out on the boat for an hour or so, and neither of them had gotten as much as a nibble on their lines. But it didn't really matter, because this was more about spending time with him than it was about catching fish. And some of her best childhood memories were of the time spent on the lake with him and her brother.

She reached for her cell phone, cursing herself again for having left it sitting on the kitchen table that morning. She would have loved to get some pictures of this day, but they would just have to do it again. She felt naked without it, and the realization surprised her. She hadn't gone anywhere without it since she started carrying one once they'd become smarter than she was.

She wasn't worried about Quinn calling since she hadn't before today. And she knew even if Quinn did call, there was no way her grandmother would answer it. She probably wouldn't have the first clue as to how to answer it anyway. Hell, sometimes Grace screwed it up, and she knew how it worked.

They'd been out on the lake for a good three hours when her grandfather opened the basket her grandmother had sent along with them. He rummaged through it until he found what he was looking for, and he smiled as he handed her a sandwich.

"I'm guessing this one's for you. I don't touch the stuff," he said.

Grace laughed and shook her head. Peanut butter and grape jelly. It was the only kind of sandwich she'd eat when she was growing up. Well, and the occasional grilled cheese. Who doesn't love grilled cheese?

"There's more coffee in there, and some water, and a couple cans of pop," he told her, waving toward the basket. "Help yourself."

Grace opened the basket and was surprised to see how much food it contained. There were all kinds of vegetables, all neatly cut and put in a tray complete with ranch dressing for dipping. Apples, oranges, bananas, and grapes. There were two more sandwiches for each of them and some sliced cheese.

"Everything but the kitchen sink, I think," she said. They both laughed, and he nodded in agreement. "When did she do all of this?"

"She gets up an hour before I do and gets it all ready for me. She wants to make sure I have everything I could possibly need in there."

"Impressive." Grace closed the basket and took a seat with her peanut butter and jelly in one hand and an apple in the other.

"She's a good woman," he said. "I think I'll keep her."

Grace watched him, knowing this was somehow going to turn into a talk about her and Quinn. She didn't mind, really.

He had a way of simply giving advice, things for her to think about. Unlike her grandmother, who liked to tell her what it was she should do. She'd always preferred having these talks with him.

"Speaking of good women…" Grace said, and intentionally let her voice trail off. He looked at her with a small grin.

"Am I that predictable?" he asked.

"Yes, you are, and I wouldn't have it any other way." She leaned over and gave him a kiss on the cheek. "It's only one of the many things I love about you, Grandpa."

He mumbled something under his breath, and Grace smiled even though she couldn't make out what he'd said. He'd always been uncomfortable when conversation turned toward emotions. He put a hand on her leg above the knee and gave it a gentle squeeze.

"Have you called her yet?"

"No." Grace didn't need him to clarify who he was talking about. Of course, she wasn't going to tell him that Quinn had called her three times the night before after the call from Callie. The first two times she hadn't bothered to leave a message, but the third time she did. Grace had expected her to leave a heartfelt message, but instead, she sounded cold and distant. Her one sentence message was etched into her mind.

Grace, we need to talk, so please call me back.

Not exactly words to inspire her to return the call. Maybe "Grace, I'm worried about you" or "Grace, I miss you, please call me" would have motivated her to call. But "We need to talk"? No conversation ever turned out well that began with those words. At least not in her experience.

"You love her?" he asked.

Grace felt a lump form in her throat and she looked away from him. She was not going to cry. There's no crying in fishing, her grandfather had always said. She nodded but didn't look at him. A week ago, she'd wondered where these feelings had come from all of a sudden, but after doing a lot of thinking, and of course actually sleeping with Quinn, she knew they'd always been there. She just wished she'd done something about it ten or even twenty years ago.

"You should tell her."

Grace whipped around to face him, wondering where his words of wisdom were. She wasn't quite sure how to deal with him telling her what she should do. He laughed at what she was sure was an expression of utter shock on her face.

"Hear me out, Grace, okay?" he asked, and she nodded her response, still not completely trusting herself to not start crying. "Life is short. Who knows where I'd be if I hadn't taken the bull by the horns so many years ago and told your grandmother she was going to spend the rest of her life with me?"

"You *told* her?" Grace managed, even though now she wanted to laugh. She really couldn't imagine anyone *telling* her grandmother anything.

"I did," he said with a smirk. "But I'm sure if you asked her, she'd tell you something different. But my point is, if I'd waited around for her to make up her mind, we might never have gotten together. Love is something you need to grab hold of and guard it with your life."

"I'm not sure she loves me," Grace said with a shake of her head.

"She does, honey, trust me." He nodded as he reeled in his line so he could check the worm he'd put on the hook. "And I think you know it too."

She took a deep breath. She thought she knew it too, the night they'd slept together, but she wasn't so sure now. She decided right then she'd call Quinn as soon as they got back to the house. One of them had to quit being stubborn long enough to answer the other one's call, right?

"I think she might be happy just being friends."

"Well, here's the funny thing about people," he said as he tossed the worm into the water and dug a fresh one out of the tub by his foot. "They change. They might think they know what they want, because it's all they've ever known, but sometimes they need to be told they want something different."

Grace nodded, happy the world had righted itself and he'd given her so much to think about. Now if Quinn would just cooperate, maybe everything in her life could fall neatly into place.

❖

"Try her again," Callie said. They were sitting in the car in the parking lot of their mother's apartment building.

"When we leave," Quinn said, reaching for the handle to open the door. Callie was relentless. Like a dog with a bone, her mother would say. Quinn was getting tired of it, but she also knew Callie was only pushing her so hard because she wanted her and Grace to be together. It was what Quinn wanted too, if she could just manage to talk to Grace and convince her.

"No, do it now," Callie said, pushing the button to lock the doors. Quinn looked at her, and Callie just crossed her arms and stared straight ahead out the windshield.

"What the hell?" Quinn said, punching her in the thigh. When Callie winced, Quinn realized she'd hit her harder than she meant to. "I'm sorry, but seriously, Callie, you're going to lock me in the car? You do know all I have to do is pull the handle and it unlocks, right?"

"Humor me," Callie said, rubbing her thigh. "It's the least

you can do since I'm going to have one hell of a bruise thanks to you."

"Fine." Quinn pulled her phone out and brought up Grace's number, but she hesitated before making the call.

"What?"

"Nothing," Quinn said with a shake of her head. What if Grace didn't want her? What if she was in Pittsburgh with another woman, and just didn't want Quinn to know about it? She shook her head and swiped the screen to place the call. She knew in her heart that wasn't the case, and if she voiced her concern, Callie would just laugh at her. She counted the number of times it rang, and she was trying to force herself to leave yet another message when she actually answered. "Grace?"

"No, Quinn, I'm sorry, but this is Agatha."

"Oh, hi," Quinn said. "Why are you answering Grace's phone?"

"Well, it's a bit of a funny story, actually," Agatha said with a chuckle. Quinn waited patiently. But she was starting to figure out what was going on. "Grace is out fishing this morning with Joe. She left her phone sitting here on the kitchen table."

"And you're at home, right? At *your* home?" Quinn glanced at Callie, who was trying to discern who she was talking to. Quinn held a hand up to quiet her.

"Of course. Where else would I be?" Agatha sounded confused now, but she took it in stride. "I would have answered one of your earlier calls if I could have figured out how this darn thing works."

"Please just tell me…is she all right?"

"She's fine. Well, a little out of sorts because things are a bit tense between you two at the moment, but she's okay."

"We seem to keep missing each other's calls. We need

to talk about some things." Quinn didn't know what to say to Agatha, but the truth seemed to be too much information, in Quinn's opinion.

"Quinn, dear, after the last time you called, I did some exploring on this phone. I stumbled across her call log, and it's pretty apparent that you've been calling since last night, and she hasn't called you back. Have I figured that out correctly?"

"Yes," Quinn said as she let her head fall back against the headrest and she closed her eyes. "Yes, you have."

"I've been thinking, and I want to run something by you," Agatha said, sounding more than a little conspiratorial.

Quinn glanced at Callie again, who was watching her intently. Without taking her eyes from Callie, Quinn answered Agatha.

"Listen, why don't you call me back from your home phone in about five minutes?" Quinn had to look away from Callie, who was protesting because she obviously knew she was going to be thrown out of the car, and Quinn was afraid she'd laugh. Somehow, this didn't seem like it would be something Agatha wanted her to laugh about. "Besides, if it's as devious as your voice makes it sound, you probably wouldn't want Grace walking in and finding you talking on her cell phone."

"Not devious, so much, more clandestine," Agatha said, sounding delighted at Quinn's suggestion. "But you're right. It wouldn't do for her to see me on her phone. I'll call you back in five minutes."

"Who was that?" Callie asked when Quinn let the hand holding her phone drop into her lap. Quinn knew she was grinning. She didn't know exactly why, but she had a feeling she was going to like Agatha's plan.

"She's not in Pittsburgh," Quinn said, trying to gauge Callie's reaction. It wouldn't surprise her to find out Callie knew where she was all along. But Callie looked genuinely stunned at the statement. Quinn found herself inordinately pleased that Grace hadn't confided in her about this.

"Then where the hell is she?"

"Her grandparents' house."

"Wow," Callie said with a nod. "I'm impressed she kept it from both of us."

"Go inside. I'll be along in a minute."

"No," Callie said. "What's going on?"

"If I think you need to know, I'll tell you when I come in. Please, Cal, just go."

She finally left, after much hemming and hawing, and Quinn felt like she'd been lost at sea for the past few days and was finally in reach of being rescued. She just hoped Agatha's plan was a good one.

CHAPTER TWENTY-FIVE

Callie!" Quinn yelled as soon as she walked in the door to her mother's apartment. She stormed into the kitchen where Callie was sitting at the table with Meg.

"Be quiet!" Meg whisper-yelled. "Mom's finally taking a nap. You have no idea how much I have to fight with her to rest."

"Sorry," Quinn said, her voice lowered. She turned on Callie and grabbed her by the arm. She leaned down and spoke into her ear. "You talked to her yesterday? What the hell?"

"Yeah, I did," Callie answered as she pulled her arm away and got to her feet, no doubt wanting to be on a more equal footing with Quinn. She stepped closer to Quinn until their chests were almost touching. "So what?"

"Stop," Meg said, standing and trying to push her way between them.

Quinn figured it probably looked to her like they were going to come to blows, but they'd fought like this since they were kids. Callie had always been smaller than her growing up, and she felt the need to get in Quinn's face—literally—in order to get her point across. Now that they were the same height, Callie was still doing it. Quinn took a step back and shook her head.

"Did you know where she was?" she asked.

"No, in fact, she even told me last night she was in Pittsburgh." Callie was still worked up, and she shoved Meg's hand away, which was pressing on her chest to keep her from going after Quinn. "Back off, Meg."

"No, not until you two sit down and discuss whatever this is about like adults."

"Relax, Meg," their mother said from the doorway to the kitchen. They all turned to look at her, surprised. "They won't hurt each other. At least not seriously."

"Mom," Meg said, giving a dirty look to Quinn and Callie. "You should be resting."

"With this racket?" She laughed. "Not likely. And I told you I'm tired of being stuck in a bed. This is what life's like with these two. You get used to it."

Meg threw her hands up in defeat and stormed out of the room. Nobody moved until they heard a door slam down the hallway.

"Maybe we should have toned it down a bit," Callie said with a grin that Quinn couldn't help but return.

"You think? We're going to scare her away," Quinn said.

"How did you know I called her?"

"Her grandmother found your name in her call log and saw the call lasted about five minutes." Quinn rolled her shoulders to release some of the tension she was carrying. "At least she's answering when you call."

"I swear, she said she was in Pittsburgh."

"Relax, I believe you."

"What's going on?" their mother asked as she took a seat gingerly at the table. Quinn was immediately at her side.

"You really should be resting, Mama," she said. "You've had three major surgeries in the past few days. Let us all take care of you for a while."

"I'm fine, but tell me what's going on. Have you heard from Grace?"

"Callie talked to her yesterday, but didn't feel the need to tell anyone about it," Quinn replied.

"And Quinn just spoke with her grandmother a few minutes ago," Callie added.

"Will you two please stop bickering?" their mother asked.

"I'm driving up there tonight," Quinn said. She turned and glared at Callie, hoping her demeanor and words would be enough to convince her. "And I swear to God, if you call her and tell her I'm coming, I will make you regret ever being born."

"I won't say a word," Callie said, taking a step back and putting her hands up as she shook her head. "I promise. So what's this plan you and Agatha came up with?"

❖

As soon as they walked into the house, Grace's grandmother told her grandfather she needed to talk to him, and they disappeared upstairs. Grace stood there a moment, wondering what was going on. She finally shrugged and took the basket into the kitchen to unload the things they hadn't eaten or drunk.

She picked up her phone from the kitchen table and took it into the living room with her. She sat on the couch and put her feet up, then scrolled through her missed calls from the day. Quinn had called four times. She was about to go back to her home screen when she noticed the last call, almost three hours earlier, wasn't logged as a missed call, but as an incoming call. Further investigation told her the call lasted more than two minutes.

"What the hell?" she muttered as she looked toward the

stairs. Her grandmother had answered her phone. She quickly hit the callback button and put the phone to her ear. After the fourth ring she was kicked to voice mail. She disconnected without leaving a message. She got to her feet when she heard them coming back down the stairs. "Grandma, did you answer my phone while we were gone?"

"Yes, dear, I did," she said, sounding like it shouldn't have been a surprise. "It kept ringing, and I couldn't ignore it any longer."

"You talked to Quinn?" Grace was trying not to be irritated by the fact she still couldn't get in touch with her while her grandmother had. Grace didn't think she would have said anything to Quinn about the things they'd discussed, but it still perturbed her.

"For a minute."

"For over *two* minutes," Grace corrected, realizing this meant Quinn now knew she wasn't in Pittsburgh. "What did you talk about?"

"Was it that long?" her grandmother asked with a shrug. Grace watched as she was putting her shoes on. "She just wanted to know that you were okay, dear. I didn't tell her anything you'd told me in confidence."

"Where are you two going?" Grace didn't miss the fact her grandfather was avoiding her as he tied his own shoes.

"We need to run to the store. I forgot something we needed for dinner."

"I'll go," Grace said, feeling suspicious of their motives. They weren't going anywhere if she could help it. "What do you need me to get?"

"You don't need to do that," her grandmother said.

"I'm going."

She got the short list of things to get from the store and left in a hurry. Why were they acting so oddly? And why would they both have needed to go to the store for just a few items? She shook her head as she backed out of the driveway and headed into town.

❖

Quinn was about to turn onto the Everetts' road when her cell phone rang. It was Agatha. Quinn cursed under her breath. She thought she'd been in the clear since she hadn't heard from her for the entire drive. She pulled over and answered the call.

"Agatha?"

"Quinn, dear, she left for the store about five minutes ago. How far away are you?"

"About two minutes," Quinn answered as she pulled back onto the road. "I'll be right there."

Joe was just walking out the front door when she pulled in. He motioned for her to wait a moment, and he went into the garage to back their car out so Quinn could pull in. He shut the garage door and walked back into the house with her.

"Okay, she should be back in about twenty minutes or so," Agatha said. "We'll be gone all night, so don't worry about us walking in on anything."

Quinn felt her cheeks flush and Agatha smiled at her as she reached out and cupped her chin. Quinn tried to turn her head away, but Agatha wasn't letting her.

"Don't be embarrassed, dear," she said. "Although you are awfully cute when you blush."

Quinn cleared her throat when she heard Joe chuckle. Thankfully, Agatha finally released her and started handing her candles.

"What's all this for?" Quinn asked.

"Romance," Joe said with a wink.

"There are plenty of these, so don't worry about using

them all." Agatha placed a couple on the kitchen counter and lit them with a match. When she turned back around, Quinn was still standing there watching her, not quite knowing what she was supposed to do with them all. "Go on, put them in the dining room and living room. Do you need me to do everything for you?"

"No," Quinn murmured as she turned and did as she was told. After lighting them she returned to the kitchen. "Thank you for this."

"You're welcome. Just know that if you break her heart, you'll have us to answer to," Agatha said as they walked to the front door.

"What if she breaks my heart?" Quinn had meant it to be a lighthearted question, but as the words left her mouth, she realized Grace really did have the ability to break her heart, and the thought scared her to death.

"Then I'm sure she'll have people to answer to as well," Joe said before pulling her into a hug and kissing her on the cheek. "Relax. And don't forget to breathe."

Quinn nodded as they walked out, closing the door behind them. What the hell was she supposed to do now? She knew this was probably going to be her only chance to tell Grace everything she'd been feeling, and she didn't want to blow it. The problem was, she'd never been this nervous about spending an evening with a woman. Ever. What if Grace decided she was done with it all? If she only wanted to remain friends? Quinn didn't think she'd be able to handle it if she did.

She walked through the ground floor of the house and shut out all the lights before going back into the kitchen. She had to admit, the candlelight did lend an air of romanticism to the house. She watched the flickering flame for a few moments before she realized they would probably need to eat something.

She looked through the refrigerator but couldn't find anything other than cheese and cold cuts. Maybe they could have a picnic on the living room floor.

She started pulling things out and putting them on a platter when she heard a car pull into the driveway. She pulled down gently on the blind covering the kitchen window and looked out through the slats. It was Grace. Quinn's breath caught in her throat at the sight of her, and she wondered how she ever could have doubted the depth of her feelings for Grace. She just hoped to God Grace was on the same page.

She quickly shoved everything back into the fridge and leaned against the counter next to the sink as she waited for Grace to enter the house. She placed a hand in the center of her chest, trying with no success to calm her racing heart.

CHAPTER TWENTY-SIX

G race slowed her pace as she walked toward the house. Something wasn't right. Why were all the lights in the house off? She shook her head. Maybe they were out on the back deck enjoying the evening. She laughed at herself and reached for the doorknob. She stopped and stared when she walked in, wondering why there were candles burning all over the place.

"Grandma?" she called as she slowly closed the door behind her. There was no response, and Grace began to panic. "Grandpa?"

Again, there was no answering call. She could see through the house onto the back deck, and it was obvious they weren't out there. She set the bag down on the floor and took a couple of steps toward the kitchen. Her progress stopped abruptly when she heard a noise coming from there.

"Hello?" she called out, the panic rising in her throat, making her voice sound higher than normal. There was no answer. She swallowed hard and licked her lips as she pulled her phone out of her pocket. "Who's here? I'm going to call the police."

She saw a shadow approaching the kitchen doorway. She tensed and gripped her phone harder. Every ounce of fight went out of her when Quinn stepped into the dining room, her face softly illuminated by candlelight.

"Please don't," Quinn said.

"What are you doing here?" Grace asked. She shoved her phone back into her pocket and took a tentative step toward her, but then stopped. She knew what this looked like, her grandparents obviously gone, and candles lighting every room, but she wanted to hear the words from Quinn's own mouth.

"I had to see you," Quinn answered. She looked unsure of herself suddenly, and Grace felt her lips curl up slightly. "I'll go if you want me to."

"No," Grace said, shaking her head. They each took another step toward the other, but then stopped. Grace wondered why they both seemed to be so nervous. "I don't want you to leave."

"Good," Quinn answered, sounding utterly relieved. "Because I don't want to go."

"Where are my grandparents?"

"I don't know. They said they'd be gone all night. This was Agatha's idea."

"I love my grandmother," Grace said with an affectionate smile.

"So do I," Quinn said. "She's a very smart lady."

"That she is." Grace finally got up the nerve to close the remaining distance and stopped just inches from Quinn. Quinn's eyes darkened with desire, and Grace felt her hands on her hips, pulling their bodies together.

"So, what is this?" Grace asked, her voice barely more than a whisper.

"Do I really have to explain it to you?" Quinn's lopsided grin made her heart skip, and Grace put her arms around Quinn's neck with a contented sigh.

"No," Grace said, her eyes taking in Quinn's lips, so full

and ready to be kissed. She played with the hair at the base of Quinn's scalp as their eyes met again. "No, you don't need to explain anything to me."

She pressed her lips gently against Quinn's and then pulled back again. Quinn made a disapproving sound deep in her throat before leaning in and kissing her. It was tentative at first, but then Quinn's tongue demanded entry into her mouth, and Grace parted her lips with a moan. She didn't think she'd ever been this aroused. The feel of Quinn's tongue sliding along hers caused an influx of emotion, and Grace had to back away from her.

"What's wrong?" Quinn asked, out of breath.

"Maybe I do need an explanation, Quinn," she said. She ran her hands down Quinn's arms and took her by the hand to lead her to the couch. Once they were seated, she turned to face Quinn. "What does this mean to you?"

"I've been a fool, Grace," she said. She looked down, but Grace placed a finger under her chin and forced her to meet her gaze. "I'm so sorry."

"For what?" Grace asked, feeling confused.

"I handled everything so badly. I panicked, Grace, and I've done a lot of thinking over the past few days. Meg's family is coming out for a few days."

Grace shook her head, puzzled by the seeming change in subject.

"What does that have to do with anything?" she asked.

"Everything," Quinn answered. She took Grace's hand and held it tightly in hers as she took a deep breath. "This is a big step because her kids? They never knew they had two aunts they'd never met. When she told me they were coming, all I could think about was wanting to share it with you. Grace, I want to share everything in my life with you."

Grace allowed herself to hope for a moment. She held

her breath, waiting for Quinn to continue, but it seemed she was done. She had to hear the words from Quinn's own lips, because she wasn't about to assume she knew what she meant. She closed her eyes briefly and squeezed Quinn's hand.

"Please tell me what that means," she said.

"I love you, Grace. That's what it means." Quinn smiled at her before looking down at their joined hands resting in her lap. "I think I probably always have, but we never seemed to be in the same place at the same time. I wanted a relationship, and you didn't. Then I was with Juliet when you decided you wanted a relationship. She cheated on me, and I didn't want to allow anyone close enough to hurt me again, so I started picking up new women every night. I kept thinking I should tell you how I felt, but it seemed so wrong to me, because we were friends. Then when you said you might move to Syracuse with Lauren, everything seemed to change. But I still couldn't seem to get past the feeling it was wrong."

"Maybe it's the right kind of wrong," Grace offered with a shrug and a smile. She touched Quinn's face and ran her thumb along her lower lip. A rush of warmth flooded her body when Quinn parted her lips and closed her eyes as she let out a sigh. "But this doesn't feel wrong to me, Quinn. In fact, this is the only thing in my life that's felt right in a very long time. I love you. And to be honest, I think I only told you I might go to Syracuse to see if this was a possibility for us. I don't think I ever thought I'd actually go. I couldn't live without you in my life."

Quinn opened her eyes, and her gaze fixated on Grace's lips. With obvious effort, she forced herself to meet Grace's eyes, and the desire Grace saw there made her suck in a breath.

"If you don't kiss me soon, I think I might die," she said.

Quinn got to her feet and held a hand out to her. Grace took it, and Quinn pulled her up and into her arms. She moaned when Grace kissed her neck, and her knees almost gave out when she felt Grace's warm breath in her ear.

"They'll really be gone all night?" Grace asked.

"That's what they said," Quinn answered before placing her hands on either side of Grace's face and pulling back to look at her. They were both breathing hard, and Quinn shook her head. "I love you, Grace."

"Show me." Grace allowed Quinn to take her by the hand and lead her up the stairs toward Grace's room. Halfway up, Grace tugged on her hand, causing Quinn to stop and look over her shoulder at her. "What about dinner?"

"It can wait," Quinn replied, wondering how she could possibly be thinking of food right now. "I'm hungry for something else."

Grace just smiled and motioned for her to continue. Once in her room, Grace shut the door behind them and slid her arms around Quinn's waist from behind. Quinn leaned her head back when Grace pulled her flush against her body. Quinn could feel Grace's breasts pressed against her back, and her own nipples tightened in anticipation of what was coming next. Grace's hands moved slowly up Quinn's sides as her mouth found Quinn's ear.

"You feel so good," Quinn said when Grace's hands cupped her breasts.

"I want you out of these clothes, now," Grace said into her ear before taking a step back. Quinn almost whimpered at the sudden loss of contact.

She turned to face Grace and her mouth watered when she saw Grace was pulling her shirt over her head. She closed the distance between them and shook her head as she gripped Grace's wrists.

"Let me undress you," she said, and Grace only nodded. Once the shirt had been tossed onto the floor next to the bed,

Quinn leaned down and pressed her lips to the cleavage she'd exposed. She reached behind Grace and unhooked her bra pulling one strap down to expose a breast. Quinn sucked the nipple into her mouth and flicked it with her tongue, causing Grace to grab her shoulders as she swayed on her feet.

Grace didn't need to say anything, because Quinn knew exactly what she wanted. She straightened and picked Grace up in her arms almost effortlessly. Grace's arms went around Quinn's neck and her fingers began playing with her hair. Quinn set her down on the bed and got on her knees before her. She undid Grace's pants next, and with a little help, got them and her panties off in one move.

Grace was leaning back on her elbows watching her, and Quinn smiled before placing a kiss on the inside of her thigh, causing Grace to moan. Quinn put her arms around her waist and pulled her closer to the edge of the bed so she'd have easier access.

"Hold on there a minute, stud," Grace said. She ran her fingers through Quinn's hair, and Quinn closed her eyes, the sensation of Grace's touch causing arousal to take over every part of her. "I said I wanted *you* out of your clothes."

"I'm sorry. Would you rather be clothed?" Quinn grinned before spreading Grace's legs further and seeing how ready she was. Without waiting for an answer, Quinn smoothed her tongue from Grace's opening to her clit, then back down again before pushing her tongue inside.

Grace cried out and a hand gripped the back of Quinn's head tightly, holding her against Grace as she pulled her tongue out and shoved it back in. After a few moments of that, Quinn replaced her tongue with her fingers and took Grace's clit between her lips. Grace jerked beneath her when Quinn began to suck gently. As her movements quickened, so did Grace's breathing, and her moans began to escalate in volume.

Quinn slowed the thrusts with her fingers when she felt Grace begin to tighten around them, but she never changed the rhythm of what she was doing to Grace's clit. Grace's hips bucked, but Quinn held on, determined to ride out the orgasm with her. Grace called out her name more than once, and Quinn smiled. Grace finally pushed on Quinn's shoulder to get her to stop, and Quinn crawled up to situate herself behind Grace, who had turned onto her side.

"Are you all right?" Quinn asked quietly.

"Yes, I'm better than all right," she answered as she pressed her butt back into Quinn's crotch. Quinn groaned and put an arm around her middle to hold her in place. "Mostly."

"Mostly?" Quinn asked as she gently bit Grace's earlobe, which caused Grace to push her ass even harder into her.

"You still have all your clothes on."

Quinn got to her feet and began removing her clothing while Grace rolled onto her back to watch. When Quinn was finally naked, she got back on the bed, but Grace pressed a hand to her shoulder when Quinn tried to straddle her.

"What?" Quinn asked.

"You're sure they're gone for the night?" Grace asked as she cast a furtive glance toward the closed bedroom door. There were many things she wanted to do with Quinn, but having her grandparents walk in on them having sex was definitely not on the list.

"That's what they said." Quinn favored her with a sexy grin, and Grace's hand relaxed. Quinn obviously saw her opening and straddled Grace, her hands on either side of her head. She leaned down so her lips were only inches from her ear. "We have all night to make love."

Grace groaned, as much at the words as from the warm breath in her ear. She placed her hands on Quinn's hips and closed her eyes when Quinn began to slowly rub her center against Grace's abdomen. She could feel how wet Quinn was and she turned her head to capture her lips in a hungry kiss. Quinn's movements quickened and Grace slid her hands up to cup her breasts, her thumbs caressing her already taut nipples.

Grace couldn't stand not touching her for another second, so she gave a quick thrust of her hips and forced Quinn onto her back. She moved a hand down Quinn's abdomen and through her heat before pushing inside her with two fingers.

"Where'd you learn that move?" Quinn asked as Grace covered her body with her own. Quinn's hands were on her shoulders and moved up to cradle her face before pulling her closer for a kiss.

"I can't give away all my secrets," Grace said. Quinn's hips bucked beneath her when Grace's thumb pressed against her clit.

"Oh, fuck," Quinn said, her hands falling to her sides as she gripped the sheets in her fists. "I'm gonna come."

Grace left a trail of kisses down her torso beginning at her jaw and ending with her lips closing around Quinn's clit. She sucked gently as she thrust her fingers deeper inside her. It only took a moment before Quinn cried out and then tensed beneath her. Grace slowly withdrew her fingers and moved back up to lie on top of Quinn again, Quinn's legs wrapping around her and holding her close.

"You're amazing," Quinn said before kissing her.

"So are you," Grace answered when they came up for air.

"We're amazing together," Quinn said with a grin.

"We are." Grace nodded and ignored the feeling of disappointment at all the time they'd wasted, because the knowledge they had the rest of their lives to make up for it far outweighed any regret.

CHAPTER TWENTY-SEVEN

Quinn was making bacon and eggs when Agatha and Joe arrived home the next morning. She hadn't been sure how early they'd be, so she was happy she'd decided to shower and dress before going to work on something to eat. Grace was still sound asleep, but Quinn figured they needed the nourishment after all the energy they'd expelled overnight.

"Good morning," she said when they walked into the kitchen. "Can I interest you in a little breakfast?"

"I could go for a bit of toast," Joe said. He winced when his wife elbowed him.

"We already ate, but thank you," Agatha said. "So I take it since you're still here that everything went well last night?"

"Everything went beautifully," Quinn replied, not able to stop her smile even had she wanted to.

"Good, good," Joe said with a quick nod. "Where's Grace?"

"I'm right here," Grace said as she walked into the room behind them.

Quinn was surprised because she hadn't even heard the water running, but Grace's hair was wet from her shower. She was wearing shorts and a tight tank top, and Quinn had to force herself to look away or risk drooling in front of Grace's grandparents.

"Good morning," Grace said to her. She walked up behind Quinn and ran a hand along her shoulders before leaning in and placing a kiss on her cheek. "Again."

Quinn felt her face grow warm even though the last word was spoken quietly enough there was no way anyone else could have heard it. Quinn turned her head and pressed her lips gently to Grace's.

"It most definitely is," she said with a grin.

"When I woke up alone, I was worried maybe you'd run off again."

Quinn met her gaze and felt a stab of pain in her chest. Hurting Grace was the last thing in the world she wanted to do. She stopped what she was doing and faced her. She wrapped her arms around her and pulled her close.

"You never have to worry about that again, baby, I promise." Quinn kissed the side of her head when Grace rested her head on her shoulder. "I'm not going anywhere."

"This makes me so happy," Agatha said. "I just wish it hadn't taken the two of you so long to realize you belong together."

"I guess I should have listened to my mother and Callie when they kept trying to push us together," Quinn said. She released Grace, who turned to face her grandparents as she put an arm around Quinn's waist.

"Or the many women who insisted they could never compete with you for my love," Grace added. "I think I always knew it deep down, but didn't want to admit it because I was sure you would never return the feelings."

"For two people who claim to have been such good friends, you certainly didn't communicate very well," Joe said with a chuckle.

"At least not as far as their feelings for each other," Agatha added.

"But that's all changed now," Quinn said, gazing into Grace's eyes. "I love your granddaughter."

"And she loves you too," Grace replied.

"We should leave them alone, dear," Agatha said as she took her husband's hand and led him out of the kitchen.

When they were gone, Quinn went back to preparing breakfast, and Grace got the dishes out so they could eat. When they were seated at the table, Grace reached out and took Quinn's hands, their fingers entwining.

"So, what happens now?" she asked.

Quinn looked at her, wondering if the feelings of anxiety would resurface, but they didn't. She smiled and let out a contented sigh.

"I need to go back home and make sure my mother is okay."

"Why?" Grace asked. "Did something happen you didn't tell me about?"

"No," Quinn said, shaking her head. "I just know she's going to be waiting, rather impatiently I might add, to hear about how things went between us last night."

"Oh." Grace gave a slight smile. "Isn't it odd that your mother and my grandparents have been trying so hard to get us to see we belong together?"

"A little," Quinn answered with a shrug. "But I guess we should have listened to our elders a bit more."

"When have kids ever listened to their parents?" Grace picked up her fork and began to eat the scrambled eggs Quinn made. "So when is Meg's family coming?"

"Later today. Callie's decided another cookout is needed to welcome them." Quinn finished the piece of bacon she'd been munching on. "When are you coming back to Brockport?"

"This afternoon, I think. Would you mind terribly if I came to the cookout?"

"You're absolutely welcome to come." Quinn leaned back in her chair and crossed her arms over her chest. "I need to introduce everyone to my new girlfriend, don't I?"

"Is that what I am?"

"No." Quinn shook her head, but she smiled when Grace gave her a worried look. "You are so much more than that."

❖

"So, when is the wedding?" Quinn's mother asked when Quinn told her she and Grace were together. Quinn chuckled at her mother's enthusiasm.

"Mama, let's take it one step at a time, okay?"

"Oh, because you need to get to know each other first, right?"

"There's no fooling you, is there?" Quinn gave her a wink and they both laughed. It was good to see her mother relaxing in her favorite recliner, but she knew the inactivity was probably driving her crazy.

"What are you doing back here so soon?" Callie asked as she walked in the front door. She walked straight into the living room and took a seat next to Quinn on the couch. "Things didn't go so well, huh?"

"Things went great, Cal," Quinn assured her. "Grace is coming home today, and she'll be at the welcome party too."

"Great!" Callie stood and rubbed her hands together. "I'm happy for you guys. I'd say I told you so, but I'm not that kind of girl."

"The hell you aren't," their mother said with a laugh.

"I'll let that snide comment go for now," Callie said with a wink. "I need to get back home and start getting the food ready for the grill. When is Meg's family arriving?"

"They should be landing about now," Quinn said with a

glance at the clock on the wall. "So they'll probably check in at the hotel and then be back to our place in a couple of hours."

"Our place, huh?" Callie asked with a grin. "Does that mean you don't want me to move out?"

"No, that is not what I meant," Quinn said with a vigorous shake of her head. "It was nothing more than a slip of the tongue."

"Sure it was." Callie turned and headed for the door. "You better not show up for this party without Grace on your arm."

When Callie was gone, Quinn turned back to her mother.

"Meg is stopping back here to pick you up to bring you to the house, right?" she asked, wanting to make sure she had a way to get to the party.

"Yes, don't worry about me. Go and do whatever you need to do before Grace gets here. I'll be fine." Her mother leaned her head back and closed her eyes.

Quinn watched her for a moment, thinking how close they'd come to losing her. She shook her head and swallowed the lump in her throat. She was just thankful her mother was still here, and doing as well as could be expected after her heart attack. Quinn didn't like Lauren as a person, but she admitted to herself she couldn't have asked for a better cardiac surgeon to take care of her mother.

"Stop thinking so much," her mother said after a few moments, but she never opened her eyes. "I'm fine, so stop worrying."

Quinn smiled, but said nothing as she stood and leaned down to place a kiss on her mother's cheek. She had no doubt she could read her mind.

CHAPTER TWENTY-EIGHT

"You aren't nervous, are you?" Grace asked as she reached out and took Quinn's hand. They were still sitting in Quinn's car in the driveway of her house. By the looks of the other cars, they were the last ones to arrive.

Quinn certainly hadn't been nervous when she'd shown up at Grace's apartment an hour ago. Within minutes of her arrival, they'd been naked and tangled in her sheets. Grace smiled at the memory as her thumb caressed the back of Quinn's hand.

"Not about being here with you," Quinn assured her. She lifted their joined hands and pressed a kiss to Grace's knuckles. "I'm nervous about meeting my sister's kids though."

"They're your nieces and nephews, Quinn." Grace smiled and leaned over to kiss her cheek. "And they're adults. I'm pretty sure you won't have to worry about entertaining them by playing Candy Land or something."

Quinn chuckled and shook her head. Grace loved that sound that emanated from deep in Quinn's chest. She sighed with profound contentment, a feeling she'd never truly experienced before.

"What?" Quinn asked, a look of concern taking over her features.

"Nothing. Just thinking about how happy I am, and how lucky I am." Grace smiled when Quinn visibly relaxed. "I love you."

"Do you think we could sneak in without anyone seeing us and head up to my bedroom?" Quinn asked, a hint of mischief in her eyes. "All I want is to spend the rest of the day in bed with you. Naked. And definitely not sleeping."

"We could try," Grace answered with a shrug. "Maybe everyone is out in the backyard."

They both got out of the car and barely resisted the urge to run to the front door of the house. Quinn hesitated and placed her ear to the door.

"I don't hear anything. Maybe we can actually do this," she said with a wink as she opened the door. Just as they got to the foot of the stairs, Callie called out to them.

"It's about time you two showed up," she said as she emerged from the kitchen. Grace turned and smiled at her, hoping her frustration wasn't glaringly obvious. "Everybody's outside. Come on and meet the rest of the family."

Quinn gave Grace an apologetic look before heading after Callie, but Grace stopped her with a hand on her forearm. She stepped closer so their bodies were touching and leaned in to speak directly into her ear.

"Hold that thought, stud," she said quietly. She felt a rush of arousal when Quinn put her arms around her waist. "I'm not expected back to the bookstore for a few days yet, so we have plenty of time to spend together. Naked. In bed. Not sleeping."

"You don't play fair," Quinn said, turning her head slightly and nipping at the sensitive spot below Grace's ear. Quinn laughed at the way Grace whimpered and thrust her hips against her.

"Neither do you," Grace said.

"Hey!" Callie called. "Do I need to hose the two of you down?"

"Leave them alone," said Meg. "I think it's sweet."

Grace finally managed to pull herself away from Quinn and felt her cheeks growing hot. Quinn took her hand and led her toward her sisters, who were just inside the door leading into the backyard.

"It's not sweet," Callie said with a grin. "It's sickening."

"Shut up," Quinn said with a backhand to Callie's gut.

"You two are so cute together." Meg smiled as she looked at them and shook her head. "I have some people who are dying to meet the two of you."

Quinn didn't move when Meg turned and went back outside. Grace tried to follow her, but Quinn gripped her hand and shook her head.

"I don't think I can do this."

"Yes, you can," Grace told her. "They're going to love you."

Quinn felt a calmness come over her at Grace's words. She didn't think she'd ever get used to the fact Grace could completely ground her with just a few simple words, a look, a touch. She was the lucky one, not Grace. She nodded and allowed Grace to lead her outside.

"Quinn, Grace, this is my husband, Craig," Meg said, and Callie laughed.

"I'm sorry, but I can't get over the fact your names actually rhyme," she said before turning back to the grill.

"Excuse her," Quinn said as she shook Craig's hand. "She was dropped on her head as a baby. It's nice to finally meet you."

"You too, Quinn," Craig said with a smile. "I've heard a lot about you."

Before Quinn could even think of a response, Meg touched her arm and motioned toward the four people sitting at the picnic table watching them. The first thing that struck Quinn was how much they all looked like both of their parents. There was no mistaking they were a family.

"Ryan, Michael, Shelly, and Lisa," Meg said as they all stood and moved closer to where they were standing. "This is your aunt Quinn and her girlfriend, Grace Everett."

Quinn was overcome with emotion as they all took turns hugging first her, and then Grace. They all settled back in at the table with Quinn and Grace. They told them everything about themselves, and Quinn took it all in. Lisa was the youngest and had just completed her freshman year at college. Ryan, the oldest, had graduated from college the year before and was working on starting his own graphic design business.

Shelly appeared to be the most enamored with her and Grace, and when they were all finished eating, Quinn finally figured out why. She looked over her shoulder at Meg, who was watching her children with a smile. Quinn leaned close to Grace and kissed her cheek before whispering in her ear.

"I'll be right back."

Grace nodded and watched her as she stood and walked over to Meg. When Meg finally looked up at her, Quinn held a hand out to her.

"Take a walk with me," Quinn said. Meg took her hand and walked with her out to the gazebo. When they were seated, Quinn spoke, but was still looking at the picnic table where Grace was laughing at something one of the kids had said. "I thought you said Craig's brother was gay."

"He is," Meg answered. "And when Shelly and Ryan both came out to us a couple of years ago, I had a really rough time dealing with it. Craig's brother was very patient with me, and it took a few months, but I finally got it. I have two children who are gay, and it has absolutely nothing to do with me or how I raised them. It's just who they are. And ever since then, I've carried so much guilt for the way Beth and I treated you and Callie for so long. I knew I needed to make amends with you, but I never knew how to go about it."

"You did an excellent job raising them," Quinn said, finally looking at her. "You're a good mother, Meg. And you have four amazing kids."

"I'm so sorry I kept them from you," Meg said, and Quinn saw she was starting to cry. "I should have listened to Mom instead of Beth about you and Callie, but I think Beth convinced me it was Mom's fault that Dad left. I blamed her for so long, and refused to listen to her about anything."

"What's happened in the past is over and done with." Quinn sighed and looked back up to the picnic table. She smiled when Grace waved at her. "I feel like I'm getting a second chance at life, and maybe our family should too."

"Good luck convincing Beth," Meg said with a humorless laugh. "I truly believe some people can never change."

"You might be right." Quinn shrugged.

Beth hadn't shown up for the party, and Quinn hadn't bothered asking anyone where she was. She'd made it painfully clear she really didn't want anything to do with her, and Quinn decided it probably wasn't worth her time or effort. Either Beth would change, or she wouldn't. Nothing Quinn could possibly say to her would make a difference. She and Callie both had thought Beth was beginning to come around since she stopped avoiding them at the hospital, but obviously, they'd been wrong. She'd only done it because their mother had insisted on it.

Meg stood to go when Grace began walking toward them. She leaned over and kissed Quinn's cheek and gave her an affectionate smile.

"I'm so happy you've met my family," she said. "I love you, Quinn."

Quinn was so shocked by the words she couldn't even think of a response. Meg laughed at her and walked back to the house.

Grace took a seat next to Quinn and leaned her head on her shoulder. "You look like you saw a ghost."

"Meg just told me she loves me," Quinn said, and she couldn't help the smile that pulled at her lips. She put an arm around Grace and squeezed gently.

"Wow," Grace said. "That's progress, yeah?"

"Yeah, it is."

"So, your mother asked me when the wedding was going to be," Grace said, sounding amused. "I wasn't really sure how to respond."

"Neither was I when she asked me the same question earlier." Quinn shook her head. Sometimes she wanted to strangle her mother. "How did you respond?"

"No, you first. What did you say?" Grace sat up straighter and shifted so she could better see Quinn.

"I told her we needed to take things one step at a time," Quinn answered with a shrug.

"Have you ever thought about getting married?"

"Honestly, no," Quinn said. "I was with Juliet when it became legal nationwide, and things between us weren't good at that point. Since then, I haven't been with anyone. How about you?"

"No," Grace said slowly. "I've never been with anyone long enough to even consider it."

They were silent for a few moments as they both seemed to be lost in thought. Quinn was surprised at how good it felt to be just sitting there with Grace, not feeling the need to fill the silence with mindless chatter. How could she ever have thought loving Grace could be wrong?

"I'd consider it with you, though." Quinn hadn't meant to speak the words out loud, but what the hell? She was thinking it, and by the way Grace turned her head and nuzzled her neck, it didn't seem to have an adverse effect.

"Are you proposing?"

"No," Quinn said with a chuckle. "Trust me, when I propose, you'll know it. You won't need to ask."

"*When* you propose?"

"What?"

"You said *when* you propose. Not if, but *when*."

"Did I?" Quinn grinned at her, knowing full well what she said. She'd worded it very carefully in her head before she'd said it. "Isn't that interesting?"

"Quinn, everyone's leaving!" Callie yelled from the deck. "Come say good-bye!"

"Don't think this means you can conveniently forget our discussion," Grace said as Quinn pulled her up and wrapped her arms around her before kissing her on the lips.

"I have no intention of avoiding that subject, or any other subject, for that matter," Quinn told her. "But right now, I want to get you upstairs, alone, so we can start living the rest of our lives together."

About the Author

PJ Trebelhorn was born and raised in the greater metropolitan area of Portland, Oregon. Her love of sports (mainly baseball and ice hockey) was fueled in part by her father's interests. She likes to brag about the fact that her uncle managed the Milwaukee Brewers for five years and the Chicago Cubs for one year.

PJ now resides in western New York with her wife, Cheryl, their four cats, and one very neurotic dog. When not writing or reading, PJ enjoys watching movies, playing on the PlayStation, and spending way too much time with stupid games on Facebook. She still roots for the Flyers, Phillies, and Eagles, even though she's now in Sabres and Bills territory.

Books Available From Bold Strokes Books

Amounting to Nothing by Karis Walsh. When mounted police officer Billie Mitchell steps in to save beautiful murder witness Merissa Karr, worlds collide on the rough city streets of Tacoma, Washington. (978-1-62639-728-6)

Becoming You by Michelle Grubb. Airlie Porter has a secret. A deep, dark, destructive secret that threatens to engulf her if she can't find the courage to face who she really is and who she really wants to be with. (978-1-62639-811-5)

Birthright by Missouri Vaun. When spies bring news that a swordswoman imprisoned in a neighboring kingdom bears the Royal mark, Princess Kathryn sets out to rescue Aiden, true heir to the Belstaff throne. (978-1-62639-485-8)

Crescent City Confidential by Aurora Rey. When romance and danger are in the air, writer Sam Torres learns the Big Easy is anything but. (978-1-62639-764-4)

Love Down Under by MJ Williamz. Wylie loves Amarina, but if Amarina isn't out, can their relationship last? (978-1-62639-726-2)

Privacy Glass by Missouri Vaun. Things heat up when Nash Wiley commandeers a limo and her best friend for a late drive out to the beach: Champagne on ice, seat belts optional, and privacy glass a must. (978-1-62639-705-7)

The Impasse by Franci McMahon. A horse-packing excursion into the Montana Wilderness becomes an adventure of terrifying proportions for Miles and ten women on an outfitter-led trip. (978-1-62639-781-1)

The Right Kind of Wrong by PJ Trebelhorn. Bartender Quinn Burke is happy with her life as a playgirl until she realizes she can't fight her feelings any longer for her best friend, bookstore owner Grace Everett. (978-1-62639-771-2)

Wishing on a Dream by Julie Cannon. Can two women change everything for the chance at love? (978-1-62639-762-0)

A Quiet Death by Cari Hunter. When the body of a young Pakistani girl is found out on the moors, the investigation leaves Detective Sanne Jensen facing an ordeal she may not survive. (978-1-62639-815-3)

Buried Heart by Laydin Michaels. When Drew Chambliss meets Cicely Jones, her buried past finds its way to the surface. Will they survive its discovery or will their chance at love turn to dust? (978-1-62639-801-6)

Escape: Exodus Book Three by Gun Brooke. Aboard the Exodus ship *Pathfinder*, President Thea Tylio still holds Caya Lindemay, a clairvoyant changer, in protective custody, which has devastating consequences endangering their relationship and the entire Exodus mission. (978-1-62639-635-7)

Genuine Gold by Ann Aptaker. New York, 1952. Outlaw Cantor Gold is thrown back into her honky-tonk Coney Island past, where crime and passion simmer in a neon glare. (978-1-62639-730-9)

Into Thin Air by Jeannie Levig. When her girlfriend disappears, Hannah Lewis discovers her world isn't as orderly as she thought it was. (978-1-62639-722-4)

Night Voice by CF Frizzell. When talk show host Sable finally acknowledges her risqué radio relationship with a mysterious caller, she welcomes a *real* relationship with local tradeswoman Riley Burke. (978-1-62639-813-9)

Raging at the Stars by Lesley Davis. When the unbelievable theories start revealing themselves as truths, can you trust in the ones who have conspired against you from the start? (978-1-62639-720-0)

She Wolf by Sheri Lewis Wohl. When the hunter becomes the hunted, more than love might be lost. (978-1-62639-741-5)

Smothered and Covered by Missouri Vaun. The last person Nash Wiley expects to bump into over a two a.m. breakfast at Waffle House is her college crush, decked out in a curve-hugging law enforcement uniform. (978-1-62639-704-0)

The Butterfly Whisperer by Lisa Moreau. Reunited after ten years, can Jordan and Sophie heal the past and rediscover love or will differing desires keep them apart? (978-1-62639-791-0)

The Devil's Due by Ali Vali. Cain and Emma Casey are awaiting the birth of their third child, but as always in Cain's world, there are new and old enemies to face in Katrina-ravaged New Orleans. (978-1-62639-591-6)

Widows of the Sun-Moon by Barbara Ann Wright. With immortality now out of their grasp, the gods of Calamity fight amongst themselves, egged on by the mad goddess they thought they'd left behind. (978-1-62639-777-4)

Arrested Hearts by Holly Stratimore. A reckless cop who hates her life and a health nut who is afraid to die might be a perfect combination for love. (978-1-62639-809-2)

Capturing Jessica by Jane Hardee. Hyperrealist sculptor Michael tries desperately to conceal the love she holds for best friend, Jess, unaware Jess's feelings for her are changing. (978-1-62639-836-8)

Counting to Zero by AJ Quinn. NSA agent Emma Thorpe and computer hacker Paxton James must learn to trust each other as they work to stop a threat clock that's rapidly counting down to zero. (978-1-62639-783-5)

Courageous Love by KC Richardson. Two women fight a devastating disease, and their own demons, while trying to fall in love. (978-1-62639-797-2)

One More Reason to Leave Orlando by Missouri Vaun. Nash Wiley thought a threesome sounded exotic and exciting, but as it turns out the reality of sleeping with two women at the same time is just really complicated. (978-1-62639-703-3)